Issue 16
August - September 2019

Lezli Robyn & Tina Smith, Editors
Shahid Mahmud, Publisher

Published by Arc Manor/Heart's Nest Press
P.O. Box 10339
Rockville, MD 20849-0339

Heart's Kiss is published in February, April, June, August, October and December.

www.HeartsKiss.com

Pleaee refer to our website for information on how to submit material for *Heart's Kiss* magazine.

Available by subscription (www.HeartsKiss.com) or through your favorite online store (Amazon.com, BN.com, etc.).

ISBN: 978-1-61242-468-2

FOREIGN LANGUAGE RIGHTS: Please refer all inquiries pertaining to foreign language rights to Shahid Mahmud, Arc Manor, P.O. Box 10339, Rockville, MD 20849-0339. Tel: 1-240-645-2214. Fax 1-310-388-8440. Email admin@ArcManor.com.

Contents

I0521355

OPENING EDITORIAL

by Lezli Robyn

While I sit here and write this, the weather is not unlike the iconic kiss scene in *The Notebook*. The sky is filled with steamy rain, sweat-drenched humans, and the intoxicating smell of a summer storm fills the beachy neighborhood. (It's no wonder I see the similarities, living in the Carolinas where Nicholas Spark's books and movies are ofttimes set.)

Not only is it the perfect weather to daydream about kissing your dream lover, but it is also the perfect weather for our writers to pen their romances—or for you, our reader, to curl up inside or on a porch swing on your screened verandah, out of the rain, and read the love stories we selected for you in this new summer issue of *Heart's Kiss*.

Harlequin mainstay, Anna J. Stewart, is back again, this time with a contemporary romance, "You Bet Your Valentine," that will show us why she is so in demand by her publishers. And Pamela returns to the world she created in "Defective" (Issue 14) about Z43217, commonly known as Zee. She has all the skills of a companion droid, the military expertise of a soldier and what it takes to be a proper spy, but she keeps failing the most simple task of passing for human. She is defective. All she wants is to be chosen, even if she is damaged, and with Kuta, she finds someone who is the first to treat her like a real girl, even if she has a mission to complete. In the latest installment, "Đamaged," will she follow protocol or her manufactured heart?

Rei Rosenquist gifts us with another of her thought-provoking romances which literally show us that love is love, in all forms—even if it takes a dimensional rift for our couple to declare their feelings. Kathryn Kelly is also back with another period piece, "Blue and Gray," and we welcome Sharon Stevens to our magazine with her touching story about a married couple celebrating their twenty-fifth anniversary, trying to find their way back to each other on a celebratory cruise.

Andrea Abedi whets our appetite this issue with a scrumptious fluffy gluten free waffle recipe that can help make any breakfast in bed more cozy and romantic, and we have our usual column by Julie Pitzel. Her You Read *That?* installment this issue, "Shame Shame Shame," discusses the expectation on our novel heroines to be perfect, or more pleasing to the reader, in order to be likeable. Yet, in comparison, it is often seen as more appealing for our heroes to be damaged, even *un*likeable, at the start of the novel, until our heroines "tame" them.

Last, but not least, we have the absolute pleasure of interviewing Christine Feehan, ahead of her next book release, *Dark Illusion*. Not only is Christine a delight to get to know (I already had been gifted a signed book by her, years ago, in return to one of only two fan letters I have ever sent to authors), but she is a fascinating person, whose talent is unparalleled. Enjoy discovering more about the person behind the (multiple) famous series of books that have swept us off our feet and find out more about the books yet to come.

We welcome you to this new issue with the warmth of summer and love in the air. I now have the sudden urge to go over to my bookcase, grab a worn Feehan hardcover off the shelf and retreat to my Amish rocking chair to lose myself in some more romance. Read well, lovers.

Christine Feehan is a #1 New York Times bestselling author, with seventy-eight published works in seven different series: Dark Series, GhostWalker Series, Leopard Series, Drake Sisters Series, Sea Haven Series, Shadow Series, and Torpedo Ink Series. All seven of her series have hit the #1 spot on the New York Times bestseller list. Judgment Road, the first book in her newest series, Torpedo Ink, debuted at #1 on the New York Times bestseller list. Christine lives in the beautiful Redwoods near the ocean on California's Pacific North Coast surrounded by family, friends and several dogs.

HEART'S KISS INTERVIEWS CHRISTINE FEEHAN

by Lezli Robyn

Lezli Robyn: Hello, Christine! It is lovely to interview you today. You are a treasure to this field and a pleasure to read. I would like to start with asking you, How did you start your writing career?

Christine Feehan: I've always written. Even as a child. Back then I'd make my sisters read my stories. I continued writing and a friend of mine encouraged me to turn in one of my books to see if I could get it published. I submitted *Dark Prince* to Dorchester Publishing and they made an offer. The rest is history.

LR: With at least 75 books in publication and 16 *New York Times* bestsellers, which book in your career was the first one where you thought, "Oh, I have made it—I now have a career as a writer." Was it because of an award you won, or a review you received, or some form of milestone achieved?

CF: Believe it or not, my first thought of being successful with my writing career came when I found one of my books in the library. I've always loved the library, even working at the local library as a teen. Seeing one of my own books there on the shelves was exciting and humbling for me.

LR: *Dark Melody* is my favorite of your books. Firstly, because I really identify with your female lead, and secondly because your heroine might have had some

major (medical) hurdles to overcome, but she was one of the strongest characters you have written. Do you have a favorite character—one that has impacted you the most, in their creation—and if so, why?

CF: Ivory Malinov from *Dark Slayer*. I thought she was so strong to overcome all that had happened to her and she went on to become a protector of all those she loves.

LR: In the same vein as the previous question, have you written a book that has more of an emotional impact on you than others you have done, and if so, why?

CF: *Dark Predator* comes to mind. As I was writing Zacarias' story I had a moment in which I thought I'd finally written a character that couldn't be saved. I wanted to save him. So, when I finally was able to, that became very emotional for me.

LR: You now have seven well-known and successful series of books under your belt, with each of them hitting the *New York Times* lists. Did you find the creative process for each of these series very different? Easier or harder?

CF: At their core, all of my books are about hope. I've never really deviated from that theme. And, of course, they are about love and a happy-ever-after. I do have to research different things for different books, so the process in that regard is the same. But, I do get into a different mind-set for each series. Even a different voice. I want each book in each series to feel different and fresh.

LR: I have no doubt that one of the reasons why you are so successful a writer is your characters are so vivid it almost feels as if they could jump off the page and enter the room. Similarly, the relationships you create between your leading characters comes across as so real—so passionate and loving, even amongst all the drama your intricate plotting throws into their lives. Do you have a specific process you use in determining how to create new the lead characters for your book, that on the surface seem so different to each other, yet end up being the perfect couple?

CF: It's important to me to be thoughtful in pairing a couple. They need to feel real to me. I want each relationship to be new and unique. Whether I start with the hero in mind or the heroine I know that character needs someone to be strong where they may be weak. They need to be alike enough that we see why they are drawn together, but different in ways that they complement one another.

LR: I have noticed that one of your strengths as a writer is your ability to create a vivid backstory for your worlds you create within our world, and also your ability to weave past lead characters from earlier books into new books as secondary supporting characters, helping create a community linking your books to each other. Was this a conscious decision at the start of your career, because it would build more readership, or your form of creating a series while having standalone stories at the center of each book?

CF: I always know where I'm going to end up when I start a series. How I eventually get there may vary, but I'm purposeful in how I develop a community, characters or theme for a series. With the family and characters I'm writing about, they have to feel real to me. That's why I think it all works. I want to feel like I know them, talk to them and I'm there with them.

LR: Your books seem to mesh romance with the paranormal seamlessly. Have you always wanted to write romance? Similarly, have you always had an interest in paranormal storylines? How did this mesh to become the genre you are seen as being one of the leading writers—if not the paranormal romance Queen of the field.

CF: I love a wide variety of genres and I read a wide variety of genres. But, I have always loved romance. I love the hope romance brings. Paranormal allows me to be more flexible with what I write. I enjoy that very much. I like being able to stretch boundaries. With contemporary romance I'm constrained by modern society etiquette and expectation. My heroes can be a bit more barbaric and assertive because they're not human. Contemporary heroes couldn't get away with what my guys get away with. LOL.

LR: You are arguably one of the most acclaimed writers in this field. What is the biggest thing you have taken away from your writing career?

CF: You should always write what you'd love to read so that you never tire of writing. You should help others when you can. You should always remember to be thankful and humble because without your readers and the people who support you, you'd not be here.

LR: As previously mentioned, *Dark Melody* had a profound impact on me, in helping me overcome some scary parallels in my life (alas, I have not met my own sexy immortal hunk). How has your readers' responses to your work impacted you and how you write future books, or changed your daily life?

CF: I can't say that reader responses have changed anything with my writing. I always feel like my characters write themselves. But, it's very humbling that my readers buy the books and show such enthusiasm. Sometimes I'll go back and read letters, emails or comments when I feel discouraged. It helps me feel inspired. And, of course, my readers make it possible for me to continue my writing career.

LR: How do you want to be remembered?

CF: I'd like to be remembered as a loving mother and grandmother. Being remembered for my writing would be wonderful, but the lasting impact of kindness and love changes the world. I'm a family person, as most people know. I think I'd like to be remembered for that.

LR: A little birdy told me that you have a new book coming out on my birthday this year, September 3rd. What is it, and what else can we expect from you in the future?

CF: Yes! *Dark Illusion* will be released Sept. 3rd and it is the 33rd book in my Dark series. We'll be learning more about mages and our ancient warriors from the monastery. Bringing these ancient Carpathians from the mountains to modern America has allowed for some humor, but also has opened up opportunities to talk about the way Carpathians are changing in a new era. Isai and Julija are a power couple and I love the magic they bring when they're together.

And the book is important to the overall arc of the Carpathian vs. vampire storyline.

LR: Thank you so very much for talking to me today about your amazing career and for sharing your thoughts and passions with our readers. I cannot wait to read *Dark Illusion*.

CF: Thank you for including me. I really enjoyed doing the interview!

Release Date: September 3rd, 2019

USA Today and national bestselling author Anna J. Stewart writes sweet to sexy romance for Harlequin's Heartwarming and Romantic Suspense lines, but paranormal romance is her first love. Early obsessions with Star Wars, Star Trek, *and* Wonder Woman *set her on the path to creating fun, funny, and family-centric romances with happily ever afters for her independent heroines. Anna lives in Northern California where she deals with a serious* Supernatural *and* Sherlock *addiction and tolerates an overly affectionate cat named Snickers. You can read more about Anna and her books at www.authorannastewart.com.*

YOU BET YOUR VALENTINE

by Anna J. Stewart

The carpet muffled Tristan Ramsey's footfalls as he made his way down the hallway of the Over the River Retirement Home. The hodge-podge pattern in the tightly woven carpet seemed an appropriate metaphor for his life these days. With a scandal brewing at his PR firm—one involving his biggest client—nothing seemed to be going right, a conclusion cemented hours ago when he received word of his beloved high school principal's health taking a bad turn. It didn't seem possible, not to his mind at least. Ms. Baxter had always been…well, indestructible.

The door to room twelve swung open as if anticipating his arrival.

"Tristan." Odette King, wearing one of her trademark Christmas cactus sweaters, stepped back and waved him inside. "How good of you to come."

"When we heard you were back in Christmas Town, we thought you'd want to know." Prudence Parker, the final spoke of the Knotty Elves wheel, cast a forlorn look to the bedroom door as if only sadness waited on the other side.

"You were right." Tristan discarded his jacket, shoved his hands deep into his pockets and rocked forward on his heels as dread clawed its way into his chest. "How is she? Mom said the doctors aren't sure what's wrong with her."

"You know doctors." Odette waved her hand as if dismissing a fly. "Always letting diagnoses bandy back and forth. June will be so happy to see you. You were one of her favorite students, you know."

Tristan managed a smile. Ms. Baxter been his favorite teacher; the kind of teacher who had taken an active interest not only in his schooling, but in his life. Ms. Baxter's small but comfortable one-bedroom apartment was just like her: compact, tidy, and practical. From the brown embroidered curtains to the lineup of photos along the far wall honoring her life-long dedication to educating the students of Christmas Town, Maine, first as a teacher, then as principal. And there he was, framed and centered, on graduation day, proudly displaying his diploma alongside his mentor. And on her other side? The dark-haired, dark-eyed girl he'd secretly called his Brown Eyed Girl laughed into the camera.

Tristan swallowed the sudden lump in his throat. Not the time, he told himself. Not when his career and future were circling the drain. As if it was ever the right time to think about his long-time rival—and life-long crush—Roxanne Prescott.

"Is it all right if I go in?" As much as he would like to catch up with Ms. Baxter's two best friends, if time was short, he didn't want to miss the opportunity to say goodbye.

"Yes, yes, of course. We were just heading down to the carriage room for a late morning snack." Odette patted his arm and motioned for Prudence to follow her. "We'll be back in a bit. You enjoy your visit."

They left before Tristan gripped the doorknob. He knocked twice before pushing open the door. "Ms. Baxter?"

"Tristan." Ms. Baxter was sitting up in bed as a queen might sit on a throne, propped up amidst pillows and a hand-made snowflake inspired quilt he had no doubt she made herself. With her sharp features, slightly hooked nose, and unwavering grey-eyed stare, she'd always reminded Tristan of a bird of prey—always on the lookout for rule breakers, class-cutters, and students in need of a friendly ear. "Is that really you?"

"It is." Hearing that her voice was as strong as he remembered eased some of his trepidation as he walked inside. "I couldn't very well not come to see you when I heard. How are you feeling?"

"Better, my boy." She held out both hands, more wrinkled than he remembered, but just as steady. "So much better now that my favorite students have come to see me."

The strength when she caught hold of him and pulled him to sit beside her settling the unease that had been circling inside of him for the past six months. *One look. One word. One comforting hand and everything feels as if it might be okay.* He should have come home sooner. Wait. Tristan's stomach dropped. "Did you say students?" *As in plural?*

"Long time no see, Tristan." The confident female voice that drifted from behind him shot him back to AP chemistry with all the finesse of a rocket launcher.

"Roxie." The nickname slipped out before he thought better of it, igniting that fiery irritation that years ago had lit his teenage dreams. How was it she'd grown prettier? She'd always been a knock-out, but her youthful figure had been replaced by a woman's curves, a woman's confidence. It wasn't the designer clothes or the expensive haircut or her precisely applied makeup. It was, just as it always had been, that intensity of appraisal that curved her lips into a kissable smile. "When did you get in from Los Angeles?" Funny his mother hadn't mentioned Roxanne was in town.

"Just before Christmas." Roxanne walked to the bed and set a glass of water on the table beside the bed. "You?"

"A couple of days ago. Mom and Dad are moving to Florida so I'm helping them pack." The suddenness with which his parents had put their house on the market still didn't sit right with him. When they'd first told him before the holidays, he'd been so preoccupied with work he'd just accepted their decision without question. The guilt and concern that had accompanied him on the trip home had only grown at the sight of the "for sale" sign in their snow-covered front yard.

"Too bad you missed Christmas. They had a snow-shoe race this year." Roxanne tilted her head in that way she had; the way that challenged without actually vocalizing one.

It took all Tristan's effort not to roll his eyes. Some things never changed. Roxanne Prescott never let a challenge—real or imagined—pass her by. He should know. He'd been on the other end of plenty of them.

"Now, don't you two start bickering already." Ms. Baxter patted the back of Tristan's hand. "This old lady's just happy to have you back where you belong."

"I don't see an old lady in this room." Tristan shifted on the bed and focused his attention on Ms. Baxter as she sipped her water. "What are the doctors saying? Is there a diagnosis? Are they running tests? What's the treatment plan?"

"If you can get that information out of her, you're doing better than me." Roxanne stood on the other side of the bed, arms crossed over her chest, the concern shining in her eyes reflective of Tristan's. She looked, not tired exactly, but stressed. Odd. Roxanne thrived on pressure. At least the Roxanne he remembered. "All she's been talking about is the town library situation."

"What situation?" Tristan asked. "Sorry. I've been packing up boxes and haven't had a chance to catch up on all the town news." Even though he'd taken a few weeks' break from work—a suggestion that had come from the higher ups at his firm—whatever free time he had he spent sending text messages and emails. Of course, only Savanna was answering him, but even her responses weren't doing anything to ease his mind.

"Oh, there was a horrible flood after the pipes froze. On Christmas Day, mind you." Ms. Baxter's lips trembled. "The structure was barely salvageable. Insurance covered most of that cost, but the inside? Everything—all the books, the computers, the furniture, even the town archives—it's all ruined. Poor Dallas Blessing, she became lead librarian a while after you two left town. She's just devastated."

"Connie Barlow has been organizing town fundraisers to replace everything," Roxanne explained. "They've had bake sales and most of the holiday festival money was donated, but they're still lacking a good chunk. Now they're having a bachelor auction. I wonder whose idea that was?" She eyed Ms. Baxter suspiciously.

"It was Odette's, actually," Ms. Baxter sniffed, but she seemed to be purposely looking anywhere other than the two of them. "Poor Connie came down with pneumonia and is still on bed rest, so the Knotty Elves are leading the charge as no one else

seems to have time. We've been trying to put a spin on it, you know, make it more appealing to a wider audience. We have a lot of single gals and fellas in town—"

"Not as many as you used to," Roxanne observed. "I heard the Bells Are Ringing Wedding Chapel is doing gangbuster business. So much so they're hiring out for more staff."

"Christmas Town has become wedding and marriage central. Who knew?" Tristan patted Ms. Baxter's hand. "The Knotty Elves have taken on a life of their own. Moved beyond knitting, have we?"

"We still like to knit," Ms. Baxter beamed, color flooding her face. "Among other things. But this auction event. It does have me worried. Me being down for the count, Odette and Prudence can't handle it without me. They're like two bickering hens vying over the same rooster. There's no peace to be had. Frays my last nerve and is wreaking havoc on my health."

Tristan glanced up as Roxanne rested a hand on Ms. Baxter's shoulder.

"Please don't get upside, Ms. Baxter. I'm sure there's a solution."

"We promised the town. The children. Oh, the children." Two fat tears plopped onto Ms. Baxter's thin cheeks. "The library is a magical place. For everyone in town, but especially the children. We can't let them down and yet—" She lifted a hand and flopped it onto the mattress. "Oh, this just breaks my heart."

"We can't have you walking around town with a broken heart," Tristan said. "Roxie, you're a whiz in the event planning world out there in Hollywood, aren't you? There must be something you can do?"

"Me?" Roxanne blinked as if coming out of a dream. "Oh, I don't think—"

"Now, Tristan. Our Roxanne's a busy career woman. She has parties and weddings to plan for fancier people than us. All those movie stars and celebrities. She doesn't have time to spend helping three old nobodies try to save the town library."

Tristan's lips twitched. And here he thought he knew the best buttons to push on Roxanne Prescott's obligation meter. "Well, if she doesn't," Tristan said, "maybe I can help. What do you need?"

"Now wait a minute." Roxanne dropped her arms and kicked out her hip. "I didn't say I couldn't help.

It would just take some…juggling and shuffling. Of course I can step in."

"Oh, would you?" Ms. Baxter clutched her folded hands against her chest. "It would be such a relief knowing you and Tristan were in charge."

"Work together?" Tristan's ears roared. His gaze crashed against Roxanne's and he once again found his panic mirrored on her face. "I'm not sure that's a good idea, Ms. Baxter. Roxie and I—"

"Roxanne," Roxanne ground out. "My name is Roxanne."

Ah, there it was, Tristan thought. The temper. The irritation. The spark. He'd forgotten how much he liked teasing her. "*Roxanne* and I are still a bit combustible, I'm afraid."

"Well, you'll both just have to set all that aside. It's about time you two learned to work together. This isn't about a competition. Or who will be valedictorian or class president or yearbook editor. It's about rebuilding the library for the children."

"She only beat me by three points on that English exam," Tristan grumbled, recalling having to sit behind Roxanne at graduation as she gave her valedictory speech.

"Three points is three points," Roxanne said. "And at least I can remember your name."

"Yes, you can, can't you?" He didn't try to stop the grin. "Even after all these years." He wondered what else she remembered.

"I also know my freshman locker combination. Doesn't mean you're special."

"Enough." Ms. Baxter patted a hand against her heart. "You're making my heart flutter. And not in a good way."

Tristan fell silent. Roxanne's jaw worked as she took a long, deep breath through her nose.

"Now." Ms. Baxter folded her hands in her lap. "We've got the bare bones of a plan put together. Roxanne, you'll find the file over there on the desk." Roxanne's eyebrow arched, but she did as suggested and retrieved the somewhat thick file. "A bachelor auction is all well and good, but we need a fresh idea, something to appeal to a wider base. And possibly lead to a bit of romance."

"I knew it," Roxanne sing-songed.

"Matchmaking again, are you?" Tristan might not have been back to Christmas Town in more than five years, but his mother had kept him apprised as to the romantic tendencies of the Knotty Elves and their posse. As long as there was a single person left in Christmas Town, Prudence, Odette, and Ms. Baxter would not rest.

"What about a bachelor services auction?" Roxanne flipped through the papers and scanned the information they'd collected.

"What kind of services?" Tristan laughed and earned a tap on his arm from Ms. Baxter. "Sorry."

Ms. Baxter cackled and the familiar sound lightened his heart.

"I mean *specialized* services." Roxanne ran her finger down the page. "You know like electrical or repair work or carpentry? I recognize a few familiar names here. A lot of them run their own businesses. Have any of these men been contacted?"

"We didn't get far enough to contact anyone." Ms. Baxter coughed and leaned back against her pillows. "It was all so tiring, and people are so busy. If you go that route, we're going to need a lot of offerings to raise the money we need."

"Sounds like a challenge to me." Tristan turned wide eyes on Roxanne. "Does it to you?"

She ignored him. "We'd better make it work quick," Roxanne said. "The auction's scheduled for Valentine's Day. That only gives us two weeks to lock all this in place."

"A smart event coordinator like you can manage," Tristan said. "Right, Roxie?"

Roxanne glared at him. "Of course I can. I'll just need you to do everything I tell you to do."

"See?" Ms. Baxter said before Tristan's temper caught. "Just like old times. Only in this instance, the town and library will win. Now. I think I'd like to take a nap. How about you come back after you've had some time to discuss. I want to be kept up to speed on everything. Lunch time works best for me. Next week will suffice." She closed her eyes.

Tristan stood, waved for Roxanne to follow him and together they left Ms. Baxter's apartment, closing the door behind them.

"She looks so frail," Roxanne whispered. "And so pale. I wasn't prepared—"

"Me, either." Tristan cringed. "Have you had lunch yet?"

"Why?" Roxanne frowned.

As much as he enjoyed fighting and bickering with her, he needed to fuel up for it. "Because I haven't, I'm hungry, and we need to get to work if we have to report in with our progress. How about Posey's?"

"Okay." Roxanne nodded then glanced back as Odette and Prudence approached. "She's taking a nap right now."

"That's good news." Prudence nodded solemnly as she approached them. "She hasn't been sleeping well these days, poor dear. Have you…?" She glanced at the files in Roxanne's hands. "Did she convince you to help?"

There was something odd in her eyes, something not quite hidden that sent Tristan's spidey-senses tingling.

"With the bachelor auction? Yes," Roxanne confirmed. "It seemed to ease her mind."

"It eases all our minds. This way we can put our attention where it needs to be. On June," Odette said. "We'll just go in and check on her. Make sure she's comfortable."

"We'll be back in a couple of days," Tristan told them. "To report on our progress."

"Wonderful." Prudence beamed. "We'll look forward to it. Maybe by then June will be up to going to the dining room." They disappeared into Ms. Baxter's room.

"How about I follow you to your dad's house and I'll drive you to the diner?" Tristan said before the silence became uncomfortable. They headed outside where the winter air blew through him as only an East Coast winter could, chilling him to the bone beneath his jacket.

"Parking doesn't seem to get any better even after the holidays, does it?" Roxanne flashed a quick smile. "That sounds like a plan. I need to check on Dad anyway."

"How's Calvin doing?"

"He fell over the holidays and broke his leg. In two places," Roxanne added with a heavy sigh. "He's never been one to do anything half-way. Anyway, I'm sticking close for a few more weeks until he's off the crutches."

"Tough time to be away from the business I bet."

"Yeah, tough time." She glanced away and winced, then turned as a mini-van pulled into the empty administrator's space. "That must be Clancy Gallagher, the facility's administrator."

Tristan looked over his shoulder toward the window of Ms. Baxter's apartment. The curtains moved, but he didn't see anyone watching. "Maybe he could fill us in on Ms. Baxter's condition."

"Exactly what I was thinking." Roxanne nodded, her dark hair spilling over her jacket-clad shoulders. "Mr. Gallagher." She reached out her hand as he approached, wiping off what looked like baby food off the front of his jacket. "I'm Roxanne Prescott. This is Tristan Ramsey. We're former students of Ms. Baxter's."

"Hello." Clancy returned the greeting with an enthusiastic handshake. "My wife Hazel's told me about you two."

"Oh?" Tristan's eyes went wide.

"Don't worry. Nothing horrible. Just the fact that there's never been a rivalry at Christmas Town High quite like yours." Clancy headed to the door. "Are you coming to visit June?"

"We just left, actually. Can you tell us anything about her condition?" Tristan asked.

"What condition?" Clancy's obvious confusion didn't make Tristan feel any better.

"Ms. Baxter's," Roxanne clarified. "She wouldn't tell us, but what she alluded to sounded serious. How long has she been bed-ridden?"

Clancy frowned and looked over Tristan's shoulder. "June said she's sick? What did Odette and Prudence say?"

"The same thing," Tristan volunteered. "I half expected her to be on her death bed when I walked into the room."

"Me, too," Roxanne agreed.

"Well." Clancy shook his head. "I'm not exactly sure what's going on, but June's been perfectly fine as far as I know. She was giving salsa lessons yesterday afternoon in the activity room."

"Salsa lessons?" Tristan looked back to Ms. Baxter's window just as Prudence, Odette, and Ms. Baxter all ducked out of sight.

"Sounds like the Knotty Elves are up to their old shenanigans," Clancy laughed. "They definitely keep us all on our toes. It was nice to meet you both. I expect I'll be seeing you around."

Tristan watched in silence as Clancy Gallagher headed inside, laughing and shaking his head.

"Huh." Roxanne planted a hand on her hip and stared at Ms. Baxter's window. "You know what's happened, right?"

"Yep." Tristan took a deep breath and caught the scent of rose and lilacs drifting off her skin and hair. "We got bamboozled."

"Bamboozled? Ha!" Roxanne scowled. "We got conned."

"Does that mean you're gonna quit?"

Roxanne turned those amazing, laser-beam eyes of hers on him. "Are *you* going to quit?"

"Nope." Tristan shook his head. "She asked for help, even if she was sneaky about it. I'm going to consider myself flattered and do what I can."

"So am I." She straightened her jacket, lifted her chin. "Want to make it interesting?"

Being conned by three old ladies wasn't interesting enough? "What do you have in mind?"

"How about a trip down memory lane?" Roxanne's lips curved and she hugged the file folders against her chest. "I bet I can get more bachelors on board for this auction than you can."

"Aren't we a little old to be making bets?"

Roxanne shrugged. "If you're afraid of losing—"

"I've never been afraid of losing," Tristan cut her off and, because he couldn't resist, brushed her hair behind her shoulder. "Not even to you. What's the wager?"

"That will take some thought." She barely flinched at the name this time as the pink rose into her cheeks. "But I'm sure we can come up with something we both want."

❖

Excitement propelled Roxanne through the diner door Tristan held open for her and instantly burned off the chill of the blustery January weather. Stomping the snow off her shoes she unwound her scarf and told herself to calm down, relax. Be careful and practical. Her initial panic at being goaded into taking over the bachelor auction event was quickly banked by the realization she'd been given a potentially life altering opportunity. Whatever else she did in the next few minutes, she couldn't let her long-time rival Tristan Ramsey know her company was hovering on the brink of complete failure. She certainly wasn't ready to admit—even to herself—that the instant she'd seen Tristan sitting beside Ms. Baxter she'd felt something inside of her tip.

It wasn't just that he had grown into the handsome features he'd been blessed with, although the beard came as a bit of a surprise. He'd always been one to catch the attention of everyone; that he had a charming personality to go with the devilish blue eyes and smiling, full lips had never escaped her notice. She'd been fascinated by those lips and had, on graduation night, in what was probably the most reckless moment of her life, decided to find out if they were as tempting as they looked. They were. Her cheeks warmed. If she let herself, she'd have to admit she'd never forgotten that kiss. Or Tristan Ramsey. Not for twelve, long, lonely years.

They'd been battling one another since the seventh-grade student council election at Christmas Town Elementary, but more than that, he'd always been there. Steady. Sturdy. Reliable. But then they'd both left Christmas Town bound for successful careers, her as an up and coming event planner to the stars and him as a sports and media agent.

Was it strange or was it fate now that her entire world was about to fall off its axis, Tristan appeared again offering—even if he might not realize it—a solution potentially stabilizing for her hemorrhaging client list and financial woes.

"There's a booth in the back." Tristan glanced at the counter, caught Posey's eye.

"Go on." Posey called as she topped off a customer's coffee, her familiar orange dyed beehive hairstyle glowing beneath florescent lights. "You're ahead of the lunch rush. Grab it while you can."

"Just like old times." Roxanne hugged Ms. Baxter's file folders against her chest and made her way around the tables and chairs and felt herself falling back in time to their high school days of study sessions, bottomless coffee, and chili cheese fries.

While Christmas Town tended to celebrate the holiday season year-round—it had, over the years, become a major tourist destination—the muted Christmas music and toned-down décor was balanced by the dusting of snow and crisp biting chill in the air. Stores, houses, and businesses would always have their halls decked to some extent. It was just the way of things in Christmas Town. The gazebo in the Town Square would adjust colors and themes according to the seasons, but there would never be any doubt, no matter what time of year one might visit, that the holiday spirit was alive and well all year long.

"How long's it been since you've been back for more than a few days?" Tristan settled in across from her, folded his hands on the table.

"A while." She hadn't realized how much she'd missed her home town until she'd crossed over its city line. The knots that had begun forming before the holidays had begun to loosen, just a bit. Just enough to breathe. "Too long. Or so Dad keeps telling me."

"I know what you mean." He flipped through the table-top juke box selection, metal panels clanging. "My mom and dad let me know, down to the day, just how long I've been away."

"Things move so fast everywhere else." When had she gotten so horrible at making small talk? Since when did sitting across from Tristan make her nervous? Probably since she saw him holding Ms. Baxter's hand and comforting their former teacher as he would a beloved grandparent or parent. She scrubbed her damp palms on her jeans.

"How's the business doing?" Tristan asked and set her teeth on edge. "You're in the middle of things out in California, aren't you? Working for movie studios and production companies? Didn't you organize one of the Oscar parties a couple of years ago?"

"I did, yes." Roxanne's stomach twisted, any appetite she might have had, waning. She'd been riding a wave of triumph at the time, exhilarated by her new partner's investment, connections, and energy. She'd been so blinded by the success and praise she hadn't realized her new partner had already begun to rob her blind. She picked up a laminated menu, once again not surprised anything, not even Posey's Diner menu, had changed over the years. Time seemed to stand still in her beloved small home town. "It's hard work but I enjoy it." *Way to skirt the truth, Roxanne.* Work these days involved endless calls to vendors and clients, all of whom were expecting to be paid with money she no longer had. The only good news was that the police were on the case and looking for Clementine Gribaldi. Clementine. Roxanne ground her back teeth together. The ridiculous name alone should have tipped her off.

Wouldn't Tristan Ramsey, mega-successful agent to one of the biggest sports stars in the country, get a laugh out of her situation; a man who was all but set for life thanks to the path he'd laid out for himself before either of them had left Christmas Town.

"You always said you were going to do big things." Tristan smiled up at the waitress who arrived to bring them water and take their orders. "Coffee, please. Club sandwich, French fries, and—"

"Apple pie for dessert. I'll have the same," Roxanne said. "Only instead of coffee—"

"A strawberry shake, extra whipped cream." Tristan grinned at her.

He remembered. She shifted in her seat and smiled. "What he said." She straightened the file folder on the table. "What about you?"

"What about me?" He reached out, pulled the folder to him and flipped it open.

"Agent to stars. Living the high life in New York. Just like you always said you would."

"I got there." With his chin down, she couldn't read his expression. "It isn't all glamour and confetti, as I'm sure you know."

"It has its moments." And what moments she'd had. "I also heard—"

"You've heard a lot for being so busy."

Roxanne took his irritation as a starting flag. "I also heard you and Savanna Bond are close to getting engaged." The bright-eyed daughter of Tristan's media mogul boss was one of those women who had put her money where her mouth was and raised countless millions for various charities and causes. Roxanne had lost track of the number of times she'd seen photographs of Savanna and Tristan gracing the society and entertainment websites. "She seems nice." *Nice?* Had she just called his girlfriend nice? Roxanne balled up her fists and shoved them under her thighs. What was wrong with her? "Are the rumors true?"

"About me and Savanna being engaged?" He inclined his head. "Not exactly. We have a...complicated relationship."

"Be still my heart." Roxanne patted her chest and forced a laugh. "Ever the romantic." His lack of reaction told her there was more to the story. "Come on, Tris. Tell me what's going on with you two. You can confide in me. We're friends."

"We are?" The surprise on his face seemed genuine.

"Ah." Roxanne swallowed and reached for her water. She shrugged. "Yeah. Sure. What else would we be?"

"That's a very good question." The way he looked at her, she wondered if he was remembering graduation night. The way she'd kissed him. The way she'd always wanted him to kiss her. Even as the thought crossed her mind, Tristan turned the file folder toward him. "Let's see what Ms. Baxter has as far as notes so far."

"Oh, well, that's easy. She—"

He held up a finger.

"Right. You can read." She pinched her lips tight. She forgot he liked to come to his own conclusions. As Tristan focused all his attention on Ms. Baxter's file, she dug out her cell phone. It wasn't the distraction she wanted, but seeing as Elmer the Elf was on his post-Christmas break from hiding from customers, it was all she had. She swallowed hard at the list of voice and emails that had been piling up. What was meant to be a week respite for her to begin to figure things out had turned into a month thanks to her father's accident. It was only a matter of time before social media began buzzing. She could literally hear the clock ticking on the time bomb of her career. She needed money. She needed to work. She needed….

Her business was circling the drain. Unless she came up with a great event, a very public, splashy event featuring big, reputation-saving names, she was done. And once she was done in this business, not even Hollywood could reinvent her. One person. All she needed was one well-connected person to believe in her. She glanced up at Tristan, heart pounding heavy against her ribs.

Problem?" Tristan asked.

"Hmmm?" Roxanne clicked off her screen and set her phone aside. "No, no problem. Everything's perfect." Her cheeks ached from smiling so hard. The relief she felt when their waitress appeared to fill their table made her knees tremble. She even welcomed the instant ice cream headache that sliced through her when she took the first sip of her shake. "So, what great epiphanies did you have while reading Ms. Baxter's notes?"

"I like the idea of the services auction. It'll draw more interest I think, and from a wider range of people. We're just going to have to come up with a lot of offerings if we're going to come close to hitting the goal amount."

Roxanne nodded. Once upon a time she could have written a check for at least half the amount they needed, but those days were on an extended hiatus. She was lucky to be able to afford her rent and that was only because she'd been diligent about her savings.

It was one thing to hold a fundraiser like this in Los Angeles; the library could have been funded in a snap. Not that people here didn't care; she had no doubt they did and would. But disposable income wasn't exactly a major commodity in small towns, not even a tourist destination like Christmas Town.

"Bidders need bang for their buck," Tristan said. "Let's stop by Christmas Town Workshop after we're done here, take a look at the message board. It'll give us some ideas on what people are looking for."

"Meet market demand. I like it." Roxanne nibbled on a fry. Christmas Town Workshop, the town hardware and supply store was considered ground central for town gossip and given the project they'd just taken on, she was in need of a good dose of information.

"We might also take a page out of the Knotty Elves' book and let word leak for potential matchmaking possibilities." Tristan set the file aside and pulled his plate closer. "For others like our three interlopers who think their loved ones need a bit of a social life."

"Keeping the spirit of the bachelor auction while also providing practical solutions for people. I like it." Surprised by her return of appetite, she began eating her sandwich and found herself nearly swooning at the crisp bacon, fresh tomato, and creamy, yet spicy mayo. "How many bachelors do you think we can find in town?"

Munching on his own meal, Tristan shrugged. "It'll take some investigating. We've both been out of the loop here for quite a while. Maybe at lunch with Ms. Baxter we can ask for suggestions."

"You didn't read far enough." She grinned and pointed to the file. "I skimmed through on the drive over. Last page. A special addendum. Filled with names I do not know. I'll reach out to the mayor and see about finalizing the actual event, make sure we've got the permits and such in order. But in the meantime, I bet I can get five, maybe ten offerings for the auction?"

Tristan arched a brow. "You really want to do that? Turn this into one of our bets?"

"Why mess with tradition?" She slurped up more shake. "A little healthy competition always makes things more interesting." It would also keep him distracted from asking her too many questions. "So? What should we bet?"

Tristan's eyes narrowed and a bit of that twinkle caught her attention. "Something tells me you already have something in mind. Come on. Out with it. What do you want from me?"

"I'm not that transparent, am I?"

"You've had that same determined look in your eye since election day in seventh grade."

"I had you beat until you brought in those double frosted chocolate peppermint cupcakes of your mother's."

His grin widened. "She still makes them every year. And I was just giving the people what they wanted. So I say again, what do you want? Must be something big. The bigger the prize, the harder you work. Like that scholarship to UCLA."

Roxanne took a long drink of shake and fought to keep her expression steady. "You got the full ride to NYU." Her scholarship hadn't covered the necessities of eating and having a roof over her head, but working two part-time jobs had put her in the right place at the right time for getting a jump start on her own business. Just like now. Tristan had opened the door she'd been searching for weeks. "I'd wager you, as an agent with a big New York firm, have an excellent client list of people needing event planning. Even beyond your personal stable of clients. Not just east coast, but throughout the country. Maybe a few overseas?"

"I know a few higher ups." Tristan turned his attention back to his meal. "I think you're overestimating my connections, however. I don't have as many contacts as I used to."

She leaned her chin in her hand and batted her lashes. "I bet you have enough to share."

He stopped mid-bite. "You want access to my client list? Why? You probably know more people in the entertainment world than I do."

Roxanne shrugged. "It's always smart to keep refreshing the customer base. A recommendation from you would go a long way to expanding things for me." She was going to need to dig out her ice skates if she was going to keep skirting the edge of the truth like this. "I tell you what." The plan that had formed in her mind on the drive to the diner took form. "If I win, you share your client list complete with contact information and give me a glowing recommendation."

"And if I win?" He squeezed an obscene amount of ketchup onto his fries.

"How about…" she tapped her chin, pretending to consider. "How about if you win, I plan your wedding free of charge."

"My wedding." His brow furrowed and he frowned. "Roxie, I don't think—"

"Roxanne." When was he going to stop that? He knew how much the nickname irritated her. "And I know, I'm jumping the gun. I know there hasn't been an official announcement or anything—"

"No," Tristan seemed to swallow hard. "There hasn't been. I told you, things with Savanna are complicated."

She waved away his protest. "As soon as there is, or even before, just plan on me being part of the engagement present." The second she uttered the words she wanted to pull them back. She was practically pushing him down the aisle and yet…her breath hitched in her chest. What was that odd tingle dancing in her blood? Was that…jealousy? Regret over the idea her childhood rival would soon be married and off the market? No. She cleared her throat and reached for her shake. Couldn't be.

He continued eating, the silence stretching to the point she was sucking up the last of her shake before he responded. "Seems to me," Tristan finally said, "that you win either way. You either get my client list or you get the publicity of having planned Savanna Bond's wedding."

It was a smart man who realized who the star of the wedding would be. Knowing she hadn't fooled him one bit, she batted her lashes. "Do you think so?"

Tristan rolled his eyes. "You forget who you're talking to. I know how your mind works, remember? Even after all these years."

She never had been able to get anything over on him. But at least he couldn't read her mind. Otherwise this would be an entirely different and embarrassing conversation. How could a childhood infatuation still feel so…real? "If you have a better idea…." She shrugged as if he didn't hold her future in his hands.

"I don't. But I don't think five or ten bachelors is making you work hard enough. Counter proposal: the first one to get to fifteen wins."

Fifteen? Roxanne gulped. Even Ms. Baxter's addendum hadn't gone beyond twenty and if they were dividing the single male-townsfolk…. "That means, in theory, we could end up with close to thirty auctions."

"We could." Tristan nodded. "All the better. It's more money we'll raise. And that is the purpose, after all. Isn't it?"

"You're not just going to sit back and let me do all the work, are you?"

"Now you really are forgetting who you're talking to." Tristan leaned his arms on the table and pinned her with a look so fierce, so intense, she felt like she was having a hot flash. "I don't do anything half way. I'm either all in or all out. You want my client list? You're going to have to earn it." He held out his hand. "Unless…."

Roxanne looked down her stomach leaping like a ten-time bridesmaid after the bouquet. "There's no unless." She gripped his hand, squeezed, and shook. "It's a bet."

❖

Incredible, Tristan thought as he gnashed his teeth so hard his head ached. Just a few hours ago he hadn't thought his life could get more complicated.

Leave it to Roxanne Preston to add fuel to the already burning pyre of his life.

She wasn't his only problem at the moment. Now that he'd spent some time surrounded by Barty, Marv, and Gus at the hardware store, he finally knew what was going on with his parents. At least he thought he did.

He clicked the latch to the two-story saltbox on Gingerbread Lane. The second he stepped inside, the aroma of simmering soup and fresh baked bread welcomed him. He couldn't get that kind of home cooking—or that amazing smell—in New York. Even in the midst of disassembling their lives, his mother didn't abandon her love of cooking. Even

while Tristan began to wonder if he'd ever really belonged in New York to begin with.

"Tristan, is that you?" His mother's voice echoed from upstairs. "Go help your father out in the shed before he lands himself in the emergency room with a hernia."

"Will do." He dropped his keys into the ceramic bowl by the door and walked through the house to the back door. He'd always loved this house with its creaking stairs and ode to practicality. It was the only home he'd known from the time he was born until he left for college. Even when he came back for the occasional visit, nothing had felt better than walking through that front door and into the warm earth tones accentuated with his mother's love of Native American art.

Now when he walked inside, when he spotted all the packed boxes and bare walls normally filled with framed photos of their family vacations, a spear of sadness shot through him. None of this seemed right. None of it *felt* right. He had yet to discover what had triggered the sudden decision his parents had made to move. Not that he hadn't tried. Then again, his powers of persuasion weren't what they used to be.

"Dad?" Tristan pulled the back door shut behind him and headed down the snow-covered stone path toward what his father had established as his sanctuary before Tristan had hit double digits. He rapped his knuckles on the door before pulling it open. Finding his father struggling with an over-sized plastic container had Tristan wondering, not for the first time in his life, if his mother was psychic. The last thing any of them needed was a trip to the emergency room.

Tristan hurried forward, plucked the box out of his father's grasp and set it on the butcher block work counter behind him. "Mom said she was afraid you'd hurt something. Why didn't you wait for me? I told you I'd be home around now."

Paul Ramsey's eyes narrowed as he reached for another box and plopped it into Tristan's arms. "Got finished upstairs sooner than I thought. We have work to do if we're going to be ready for the movers. How's Ms. Baxter doing?" A big man, well over six feet, his father had always reminded Tristan a bit of Santa with his neatly trimmed white beard and increasingly jolly, if not pudgy, stomach.

"Better than expected." Tristan popped the lid off the first box and dropped into the past. "My old models. Remember how we'd sit out here for hours putting these together?" He lifted out one of the spaceships he'd saved up his lawn mowing money to buy. "I think I can still smell the glue fumes."

"Those models and that glue are why I installed windows that open," Paul laughed. "You take what you want. As much as I love them, they won't fit in the new condo."

"Yeah." Tristan winced, put the lid back on the box. He didn't have much room in his small apartment back in New York, either. He set the box aside. "I'll start a pile. Maybe keep the stuff I need to go through out here?"

"Works for me. You want any of the power tools—"

"I know about you losing your pension."

Paul grunted as he moved another box along the metal shelves. "Figured it was just a matter of time before you heard."

"Why didn't you tell me?"

"Nothing you can do about it, son. Nothing any of us can do except move on."

He couldn't believe his father's cavalier attitude. They were talking about selling the family home; the only home he'd ever known. "Dad, the mortgage can't be bad enough you have to sell and move. If you and mom need money—"

"We aren't charity cases. And I won't have my son bankrupting himself because I've made some poor choices. Now are you going to help me with these boxes or not?"

There had to be more going on here. What weren't they telling him? "Are you sick?" The question alone made him feel ill. "Or mom? Is there something wrong?"

Paul sighed, but kept his back to Tristan. "It's nothing like that, son."

"You sure? Because this, none of this feels right to me. If neither of you is sick, then the only other thing it could be is money. Dad, I have some stashed away. I can help—"

Paul turned and rested his hands on Tristan's shoulders. "I know your default setting is to help and fix things, but some things can't be fixed. As much as we love Christmas Town, we've come to terms with this. Your Aunt Enid owns a number of

condos in Miami and we're actually helping her out by taking one off her hands. You being here to help us move is help enough. It'll be fine, Tristan."

No, Tristan thought. It wouldn't. But he knew when his father had ended a conversation. Which meant he was going to have to find out the truth another way. "You'll never guess who I saw today at Ms. Baxter's. Roxanne Prescott."

"Really?" Paul didn't look nearly as surprised as he sounded. "I think I'd heard she was back in town. How is she?"

"Good. Successful, of course." Distracting as ever. Tempting. He couldn't believe his teenage crush had been reignited. "Ms. Baxter asked us to take over running the town bachelor auction for Valentine's Day. You know, to raise money for the library."

"Terrible shame about the flood," Paul said. "But I always thought you and Roxanne could get a lot more done working together than you could fighting for first place. So did Ms. Baxter, if I remember correctly. Must be a sign, the two of you being back here at the same time." Paul hefted another box down and sorted through the various wood working and handyman tools.

It was his father's past, Tristan thought. All those weekends he'd spent fixing up the house, the pride the former factory manager took in the house he and his newlywed wife had moved into over thirty years ago. There wasn't an inch of this house that didn't hold a memory or reminder of what a great childhood Tristan had been blessed with. What a good life his parents had had here. And now, for some reason, they were simply walking away? He might not be able to do much to salvage his job, but he could darn sure make certain his parents were taken care of.

"We'll need a place to work. We could meet at the diner, but I'm not sure my cholesterol can take it." Tristan wandered the space, pushing aside the thoughts of what would be going to charity and what would be simply thrown away. "Can we use the shed?"

"Fine with me," Paul said. "As long as you don't mind the boxes. Take care to go through stuff, though. I don't want you regretting not taking what you want."

"I will," Tristan said. "If you're about done, I think dinner's going to be ready."

"Beef barley soup." Paul beamed over at him. "That mother of yours never fails to warm up a chilly day. Just help me move a few more of these boxes off the shelves."

Later, after dinner, and up in his old bedroom, Tristan flipped through the photographs he'd taken of Ms. Baxter's file on his phone. Her initial list along with the postings of job offerings and business services available they'd found on the bulletin board at Christmas Town Workshop gave them a great jumping off point. He could only hope there was enough interest in town for him to hit fifteen bachelors. Who was he kidding? There had to be interest enough for at least double that since there was little chance Roxanne was going to do anything other than go full bore.

He had to win. He couldn't share a contact list filled with people who were not taking his calls. Not that he was in a position to come clean about the true nature of his relationship with Savanna Bond. She'd pleaded with him for more time, to let their relationship continue to play out in the press while she figured some things out. Still, the situation with Savanna would be easier to explain to Roxanne than him having lost all professional credibility.

So…yeah. For once, losing to Roxanne Prescott was simply not an option.

❖

At close to noon the next day, Roxanne walked up the steps to the front door of the Ramsey house, her nerves clanging almost as loudly as the doorbell when she rang it. The woman who opened the door smiled that familiar, warm, welcoming smile that had greeted Roxanne many times during her childhood.

"Roxanne." Helene stepped out to give her a quick hug before ushering her inside. "I'm so glad we got to see you before we left. I'm tempted to ask if you've come over to study with Tristan."

Roxanne's face went hot, but she scooted past Tristan's mother before she saw. "Hi, Mrs. Ramsey."

"Oh, it's Helene, Roxanne, please. You're all grown up now. We're more like old friends, aren't we?" Helene swept her down the hall into the kitchen where rolls of bubble wrap and boxes awaited them. "Forgive the mess. Moving after more than thirty years means there's quite the clutter to deal with."

"I'd heard you were moving." Roxanne set her files and notes on the table, hooked her purse over one of the high back chairs. "Florida, is it?"

"Yes." Helene nodded, keeping her chin down. "We're about to be condo owners."

"Well, Christmas Town isn't going to be the same without you," Roxanne said. Just another piece of her childhood that was disappearing. She hadn't realized, until she came back, just how much she'd missed this place, including this house. She and Tristan might have been rivals, but she'd spent a good amount of time in this house growing up. There was no one better to study with than the person who challenged you most. She'd found the Ramsey home a particular refuge after her mother died; with her father working such long hours, she'd liked spending time with Helene, who had also been one of her mother's best friends. "If there's anything I can do to help, I hope you'll let me know."

"That's sweet of you. Thank you, Roxanne. I think Tristan stole the extra coffee machine for the shed."

"He texted me last night and said he was setting up shop for us in there. Just like old times." The memories collided as she headed outside to the shed. Who would have thought her future would depend on winning Tristan Ramsey's contact and client list? And it did. More than ever. She'd spent the morning on the phone with her lawyer discussing the threatened lawsuits from at least two former clients and one vendor. She needed to get some cash rolling in and fast.

Her hand stopped before she knocked on the door. She could hear Tristan's raised voice through the thin shed walls.

"Sorry I'm late." She found him sorting through an old grey plastic container, lining up detailed models along the back counter. His red plaid shirt stretched across broad shoulders. When he glanced back and she caught a glimpse of the beard, she could barely think of him as a media agent. He looked as if he belonged on one of those reality TV shows about woodsmen or lumberjacks.

"Morning. There's coffee over there." He returned to his models while she unloaded her things and poured coffee into a chipped Mighty Mouse mug.

"Thank goodness." When she sipped, she sighed and earned another smile from him. "Dad's gone decaf on me and I didn't have time to stop at the Tea Pot for take out." She sank against the counter and cradled the warm mug between her hands. "You make a good cup."

"One of the first things my dad taught me. A talent that has saved my life on more than one occasion."

"They have you making a lot of coffee in that New York high rise of yours?" She'd meant to tease him, but instead of earning a glimmer of a smile, his gaze barely flickered.

"How much did you hear?"

She shrugged. "Enough to know things aren't as rosy as you've made them out to be."

"Please tell me you aren't about to gloat. I'm not sure my ego could take it at the moment."

"I'm not gloating." She'd never seen him look so… what was the word? Defeated. There was a time she might have basked in his failures, but not now. Not when she knew what it was like to be on the receiving end of bad business news. And not when she saw how unhappy he was. "Is it just work or is there something else?"

"Like what?"

"Your parents." She knew how she'd felt seeing that for sale sign in the front yard. She could only imagine, or maybe she couldn't, what he must be feeling. "Their move can't be easy for you. I know how much you love this house. How much Christmas Town means to you."

"Yeah, my parents." He scrubbed a hand down the side of his face to the back of his neck. "You probably knew about the factory pension issues."

"No, actually." Her eyes went wide. "I'm sorry. What happened?"

"I don't know. Dad doesn't want to talk about it. What I do know I got from the three wise men at Christmas Town Workshop. It doesn't make any sense. The mortgage on this place should almost be paid off. They shouldn't have to sell it and move to Florida."

"Maybe your mom will tell you."

Tristan shook his head. "If Dad won't say, she won't. They're always in lock step with each other."

"I could ask my dad. Maybe he knows." Roxanne had been preoccupied with her business she hadn't had much time to just sit down and talk with her dad, especially not when he was cranky and grumbling about his broken leg. "Can't hurt."

"That would be great, thanks." Finally, a touch of a smile curved his lips.

"I understand, you know. The work stuff. How it can sometimes feel like an avalanche falling on your head. Believe me, I do."

"I find that hard to believe. I've snagged an old white board from the garage." He turned and hefted the board onto the counter beside the window as if changing the subject. "Thought we could keep track of our progress on it."

"Okay." She shrugged out of her jacket, trying to come up with the words that had been confusing her since their lunch at the diner. "You know, something you said yesterday left me thinking."

"I made you think? That's a first."

She wanted to laugh. She wanted to think it was a joke, but unease prickled along her shoulder blades and fed the gnawing doubt she'd fought against. "You always made me think. You always challenged me. I guess I thought that's why we were friends but…we aren't, are we?"

"Would that bother you?" Tristan's question was one she'd been asking herself for the past day.

"Yes, actually." Although she wasn't sure why. "You were a big part of my childhood. A vital part. I don't know I could have gotten to where I am if you hadn't been driving me."

"Ditto."

"Seems to me two people who grew up together the way we did should be friends."

"You'd think." He drank his own coffee. "I just never figured you saw me as anything other than a test score to beat."

She'd seen him. She hadn't realized how clearly until yesterday at Ms. Baxter's. She'd missed him. It was almost as if this odd, empty space inside of her suddenly filled, loading her up with more optimism and hope than she'd felt in a long time. Not that he needed to know that. Not that he'd understand. "There's something to be said for a man's test scores."

He shook his head. "Always with the joke."

Because jokes kept things light. Jokes kept conversations from getting too serious or shifting toward topics she didn't want to discuss or think about. Jokes, along with rivalries, kept people, kept *him* at a distance. Her life might be topsy-turvy at the moment, and the last thing she needed was to admit to herself she'd come to see him in a way that wasn't practical or convenient for either of them. Not that there could be anything now. He was, after all, an almost engaged man. But clearly she wasn't the only one going through something. Maybe…maybe she needed to focus on something, someone, other than herself. "I've thought about you a lot over the years. Wondered how you were doing, other than what I read online. I almost emailed you a couple of times, you know, to touch base." She drank some of her coffee. "I told myself you probably wouldn't answer."

"You were wrong."

"What's going on here?" She set her mug down, unable to stand this odd, strained tension between them. This wasn't what she remembered and it certainly wasn't what she wanted. "Why are things so… weird between us?"

"Because we aren't teenagers anymore."

"That's not it." That made it sound too simple and yet…they weren't, were they? "We're the same people—"

"No." Tristan shook his head. "We aren't."

"Right." She forced a laugh, tucked her hair behind her ears. "I guess instead of being obsessed with our grades and beating each other, we've focused on our careers and, well, other stuff." And it seemed as if they were both suffering for it. Priorities. When had she messed hers up so miserably?

When his grin reappeared, she felt those knots in her stomach loosen. "Other stuff?"

"You know. Personal stuff. You have an almost fiancée and I…" don't. Other than a failing business and lawsuits hanging over her head, what exactly, did she have? A longing to be someplace that felt like home. Felt right. Instead of her spending every minute of every hour trying to fit in to a place and world that seemed far too eager to kick her out. Fear percolated with uncertainty, brewing stronger than the coffee in her mug. Had she ever really belonged anywhere other than Christmas Town?

"You what?"

She inched up her chin and beamed. "I've been thinking of starting a relatively long-term relationship with a goldfish."

"I seem to recall you don't have the best of luck with fish." His smile widened and she took that as a

success. When he stepped closer, she had the oddest impulse to meet him half-way.

"I'm all grown up now. I'm much more responsible." The word almost caught in her throat. If she'd been responsible, she wouldn't have turned so much of her business over to someone else. Someone who obviously could not be trusted. She could feel the warmth of his body, almost feel the brush of his touch, his fingers against her skin. She squeezed her eyes shut, just for a moment, as if rebooting her system to remind herself he was with someone else. "Is Savanna going to be joining you while you're here?"

"You seem oddly preoccupied with her. If you're thinking about trying to get her on your side of the bet—"

"I wasn't." Geez. She winced into her mug. "I'm not really that bad, am I? Was I?"

He shrugged. "As much as I'm enjoying this odd skip down memory lane, we should probably get to work." He handed her a marker. "I assume you already have a chart in mind."

She did, but for some reason, she wasn't as proud of it as she had been earlier this morning. "I was playing around with something."

"Great. Have at it. I'll just finish up with these boxes. Just tell me when you're ready for my input."

He really did make her sound like an utter control freak. But she began marking up the board anyway. By the time she was done scribbling, he'd set the last box on the metal shelf and joined her at the long, narrow counter. "I'm thinking we can divide up names—maybe draw them out of a hat so it's fair?"

"Works for me." He retrieved a metal bucket while she cut up the copy of the list Ms. Baxter had made and dropped the names inside. "We flipping for who goes first?"

"You can go first." She pushed the bucket toward him then reached out, touched the back of his hand. "I'm sorry."

"For what?"

"I must have really been a nightmare. You probably deserve a medal for putting up with me."

"You knew what you wanted, and you found a way to get it. I admired your determination, actually. It pushed me to do better. I can't blame you for it."

"Yeah, well, maybe you should." Maybe if she'd learned that lesson sooner, she wouldn't be in the professional mess she was in now. There was a difference between having high standards and being a controlling, obsessive, nit-picky…well, she knew what her reputation was. "Maybe if I'd still had you in my life things would have turned out differently. You were always a good check." A check she'd never had from anyone else. "You always told me when I was going too far."

"Roxanne—"

"I meant what I said, Tristan." If she didn't get this out now, she never would. "I'm sorry. I should have been a better friend. I should have seen what a good one you were to me." She heard him release a breath, but she kept her attention on the scraps of paper in the bucket. "But I understand if—" She inhaled deeply. "I understand if you can't accept it."

"Of course I accept your apology. I am, after all, the bigger person."

"Yes, you are, aren't you?" She knew he was teasing her again, and when she looked up she found him close. So close. Too close. There was something different in his expression, something she couldn't have expected—only hoped for. Reason vanished. She moved in, rested her hands on his shoulders and pressed her lips to his.

Her head spun. Her body turned warm when he gently, slowly, lifted his hand to her face and kissed her back. All these years, she'd tried to forget how he'd made her feel, as if being in his arms was the only place she belonged. She couldn't. She hadn't. And yet….

She broke away, shame and guilt washing over her as she pressed her lips together to cling to the taste of him. "I'm sorry. That was wrong. Inappropriate. I shouldn't have—"

"Roxie." He reached for her, his beautiful eyes softening in concern. "It's all right. It's more than all right. I wanted—"

"No." She pressed her hands against his shoulders and pushed herself back. "No, please don't embarrass me any further. That never should have happened. It won't. Happen. Ever again." She didn't know her face could feel this hot. She cleared her throat, blinking back tears of humiliation. She'd kissed an engaged man! What was wrong with her? "Let's get back to the auction, all right? Please. Draw your first name."

"Roxanne."

How she loathed the sympathy she hard in his voice. She squeezed her eyes shut. "Please, Tristan."

"All right." He turned back to the white board and plucked a slip of paper out of the bucket. "Back to business. Kevin Dennings. I remember him from high school. Consider him in."

"What's going on with you two?" From across the dining table in the Carriage Room at Over the River, Ms. Baxter pinned Tristan with that all-too familiar and assessing look while Roxanne excused herself from lunch.

"Nothing," Tristan said. "Just working together like you planned."

"Mmmmm." Odette scrunched her mouth to the point it almost disappeared. "Doesn't seem like it's going to plan to me."

"Hush." Prudence must have kicked Odette under the table because Odette jumped, some of the glitter from her flowered Valentine sweatshirt falling onto the tablecloth.

"It's not like he doesn't know. They both do. Because they have eyes." Odette sighed and cast a forlorn look at Ms. Baxter. "I told you it wouldn't work."

"You told her what wouldn't work?" Tristan looked among the three elderly ladies, then glanced around the suddenly quiet dining room where the other residents of the facility seemed interested in the answer. "Were you playing matchmaker with me and Roxanne, Ms. Baxter?"

Ms. Baxter shrugged. "What if I was? You two are two of a kind. Never had two students who were so well matched. All these years I assumed the two of you would figure it out."

"Well something's going on. They aren't speaking to each other."

"We're speaking to each other just fine." About the auction at least. Any other topic it seemed had been deemed inappropriate after she'd kissed him in the shed four days ago. He'd welcomed the distraction of considering the shift in his and Roxanne's relationship, no mater how uncomfortable things felt. It was certainly preferable to the latest round of emails that had proven Tristan's suspicions that his client's latest endorsement deal was about as bad as he'd warned. "We both just have other stuff going on."

"Other stuff, pah." Prudence sniffed at her recently arrived salad. "You two keep lollygagging around you'll break our streak."

"What streak?" The second he asked he wished he hadn't.

"You and Roxanne would make fourteen couples we've unified in wedded bliss." Odette announced proudly. "We're aiming for twenty by the end of the year."

"Are you?" Tristan couldn't help but be amused. "And you all deemed me and Roxanne worthy of your attention? I'm shocked."

"No, he isn't." Prudence pointed her fork at him. "You're humoring the old women."

"Okay, so I'm not shocked." How could he be when the matchmaking antics of the Knotty Elves made the town newspaper. "But I am touched. And while I appreciate the vote of confidence—"

"See?" Ms. Baxter sat up straighter in her chair. "I told you. He's smitten. Always have been, haven't you, Tristan?"

"Yes, ma'am." No point in denying it now. He was fast losing patience with and for secrets, especially his own. "But now that you've managed to put me and Roxanne in the same vicinity, how about you let me handle the rest of it. There are some elements to both our lives that make things a bit complicated."

"Why is love always so complicated for young people?" Odette asked as if Tristan wasn't sitting right there. "They make everything so difficult. You're crazy about the girl. She likes you. What's the problem?"

"The problem is we each have lives outside this town. Lives we can't just walk away from on a whim."

"Who's talking whim. Think it out, young man," Prudence ordered. "Better yet, think of the possibilities. You and Roxanne have worked wonders on the auction. The list you've come up with, all the organizing and planning, the town library'll be funded before we know it. And we'll have you to thank."

"Even if we were bamboozled into taking over for the three of you."

None of them looked remotely ashamed. "Not going to apologize for a plan that worked." Ms. Baxter sat back as her lunch was placed in front of her. Tristan accepted the same meal, roast chicken with gravy, mashed potatoes and bright steamed carrots dotted with parsley. "You still have work to do, though. I expect a ring on that girl's finger before I check out of this place."

"You aren't going anywhere, and you know it," Tristan said. "And stop threatening us with that. You fooled us once, not again. You'll probably outlive everyone in Christmas Town." Especially if Roxanne kept kissing him. He'd often wondered what it would take to stop his world from spinning, and she'd done just that the second she'd pressed her lips to his. All these years he'd thought graduation night had been a fluke, but nope. Not even close. Too bad he was prevented from doing anything about it because of a promise to a friend. But that wouldn't be the case forever. At some point, hopefully soon, Savanna would feel secure enough in her choice to set things right. In the meantime….

In the meantime, he'd watch Roxanne make her way back to the table, her snug jeans and eye-popping yellow t-shirt a treat for his eyes. She really had no idea how she came across. How she made people smile with her open expression and friendly gaze. Even with the exhaustion he saw creeping across her face in recent days, he still thought she was the most beautiful woman he'd ever seen.

"See there? That." Ms. Baxter smiled so wide her eyes almost vanished. "There's the look. Took you long enough."

"Took who long enough to what?" Roxanne reclaimed her chair between Odette and Prudence and, purposely avoiding glancing at Tristan, plucked up her fork.

"Oh, you'll find out soon enough," Ms. Baxter sang.

"You're not about to con us into another job, are you?" Roxanne sighed that heavy play sigh Tristan had come to appreciate. "Because we still have our hands full with the first one."

"Don't we know it," Prudence agreed. "But don't worry. All is well. Or all will be well. Eventually."

Roxanne frowned, finally looking to Tristan for answers. He simply shrugged, toasted her with his water glass, and continued eating.

❖

"Sorry I'm late."

Tristan jumped as Roxanne slid into the booth across from him, waved to Posey for some coffee. "I didn't notice." He turned his phone over, moved it out of reach. It had been ten days since the two of them had reconnected. Just over a week since she'd kissed him in the shed. One very long, very thought-provoking week. It had taken her that long to stop avoiding any topic that didn't involve bachelors or auctions. For the most part at least.

She shrugged out of her jacket and settled in, setting her ever present folder on the table beside her. "I need to get something off my chest." She leaned her arms on the table.

"Go for it."

"I kissed you."

He nodded. "I remember." Vividly. "It's happened twice, actually."

"I think I know why."

He hoped he did. "Do tell."

"I haven't been completely honest with you. About my business. And what's going on. And I decided today that you need to know the truth."

Great. The truth. Because he was on such great terms with it himself.

"I hit a bit of a rough patch where the business is concerned. A few months ago. Well, just after Thanksgiving."

"I'm sorry to hear that." More sorry than she could imagine. "What's going on?"

Even though she'd brought up the topic, she seemed hesitant. "There's really no way to explain without showing what a complete idiot I was. I have—had—a business partner. Clementine Gribaldi."

Tristan nearly spit out his coffee. "I'm sorry. Clementine?"

"I know." Roxanne held up her hand and rolled her eyes. "The TV movie kind of writes itself. Anyway, to make a long story short, she invested pretty heavily, then after a few years, took off with most of our operating cash. She just took off, leaving me to deal with bills from vendors who hadn't been paid and contracts for events I didn't know we'd taken on. It's…." Roxanne tucked her arms around herself. "Well, it's all been a bit of a disaster. Or it was until I saw you."

"Me." Dread descended, thick and stifling.

"I told you all I need is one big recommendation to get me back in the game. One word from you and your agency, or say one big event like your wedding and I'll have my chance. So, yeah. You were right. Win or lose this bet, I win. And I can't thank you enough." She reached out and grabbed hold of his arm. "You have no idea what the opportunity means to me."

"And that connects to you kissing me how exactly?" Even before she answered he felt his spirits droop.

"Gratitude of course. And relief. I should have realized that sooner. All the warm fuzzy feelings had to be coming from there. I mean, what kind of person would I be if I went after a man, a friend, who was getting married to someone else?"

Gratitude. That's what she'd come up with. Was now the right time to tell her she couldn't lie to save her life? He saw the doubt in her eyes, the hope that he'd believe her clinging to that hope. The hope that he was the answer to all her problems.

"Roxanne." He looked down at her hand, felt the warmth of her touch through the fabric of his shirt. "I don't think you should get your hopes up. I'm not sure my name is going to bring you what you need."

"Of course it is! You're pre-engaged to Savanna Bond!" She leaned back when Posey brought their food. "You have to know the prestige being mentioned in the same sentence as her will give my company. That alone might be enough to give me some time to get back on my feet."

Pressure built up in his chest. He'd known the fall-out from his client Harrison Russo's endorsement fiasco would be extensive, but no way could he have anticipated it having such a far reach. If only Russo, an up and coming basketball superstar, had heeded his advice about not signing an endorsement deal with the start-up sportswear company. If only the kid had looked beyond the dollar signs and fast cash and waited for the investigator Tristan had hired to finish his examination of the company finances and short history. If only the company's stock hadn't exploded last week once news of the deal broke. And oh, if only the deal hadn't triggered a more scrupulous examination of the company by various media outlets. Outlets that uncovered the company in question was under investigation in not one, not two, but *three* countries for running sweatshops that employed children as labor. Given Tristan's client's main focus outside the court was youth programs and education, the publicity disaster wrote itself. With Tristan's agency caught right in the middle.

Now, because Tristan hadn't pushed harder to be heard, hadn't pushed his client harder not to sign, not only was his own career about to tank, it could very well drag Roxanne's along with it. He should have told her the truth from the start. He never should have let her get her hooks into this dream of hers that he was going to be able to save her. Save her business. His client list may as well have ended up in the office shredder and his wedding to Savanna…he'd really dug himself into a hole.

"Roxanne, I think you and I need to talk about a few things. Important things."

"Yeah, we will, we will. I just needed to get that out. Whew. I feel so much better."

She looked as if she did. Some of the color came back into her cheeks and her smile had returned. A smile she no longer had any problem aiming in his direction. He didn't want to dim that light in her eyes. Not for anything.

He might not have any clout left in New York, but he still had his word and he'd promised to stand by Savanna's side as long as she needed him.

In the meantime, he'd remain caught in an increasing tangle of his own lies, trying to protect his friends, his family, and his own reputation. And there, in the middle of it all, was the girl he'd never gotten over. And when she found out the truth—when she found out he'd been lying to her from the moment they'd reconnected…the idea made him slightly sick.

"Tristan?"

"Yeah?" She was looking at him as though expecting him to answer. "Sorry. Did you say something?"

"I just said I had some interesting developments this morning as far as new auction offerings. How about you?"

"Sure. Right." He leaned over and pulled out the notebook paper he'd been using to keep track of his acquisitions. "I went up the Blue Spruce Ski Resort after breakfast."

"Blue Spruce, got it." Roxanne bent over her chart and filled in another box for him. "I heard they'd reopened that a few years ago. Who did you get?"

"Ryan Reeves, one of the ski instructors. He'll offer skiing lessons, either this season or next."

"Excellent. Anyone else?"

"Yeah. Rob Rahily wants to throw his name in. He's going to let me know the details, but he's has serious carpentry skills, so I'd expect something along those lines."

"Great. So that brings you up to…seven." Her grin almost reached her ears. "I ran into Aiden Moretti's grandmother. Although, if I had to guess, I'd say she hunted me down. She's gotten him to offer a private plane ride to Portland along with dinner and dancing. I think she's hoping serious sparks will fly for him. So to speak."

"Nice." Tristan glanced up and nodded his thanks as Posey refilled his coffee. "How are you doing, Posey?"

"Can't complain. How are you two coming along with the bachelor auction? Anyone in my age range offer himself up yet?"

"I've got Gus offering up chess lessons." Roxanne leaned her chin in her hand.

Tristan hid his smile behind his mug. Gus was one third of the trio of elderly men who held court at Christmas Town Workshop and probably rivaled Santa himself in the age game. Nothing, absolutely nothing, happened in Christmas Town without the three wise men hearing about it.

"Where Gus goes, you know those two friends of his will follow. Don't know that I'm up to that," Posey sighed.

"How about Abel Billingsworth? He's contributing a landscape design for both a front and back yard."

"Landscaping is why I cemented in my yards. Keep us older folks in mind, would you? I don't need half-in the grave, mind you, but I do like a silver fox."

"Ms. Baxter might have some ideas on that front," Tristan assured her.

"You two want your usual for lunch?" Posey asked.

"Please." Tristan didn't need to check with Roxanne. They'd fallen into a routine he'd begun to enjoy; a routine he'd thrown himself into now that his parents were just about finished packing up the house.

"What other interesting conversations did you have today?" He asked Roxanne once Posey went to put in their order.

"I finally tracked down Gage Flannigan. He agreed to offer a day of handyman services. This one will probably bring in the most as everyone always needs some help around the house."

"Which brings you up to nine." Tristan tried not to sound completely defeated. Losing meant admitting the truth about his situation sooner than later. "I did run into a couple of interested parties on my way to the diner. I need to confirm his participation, but I thought you'd get a kick out of this." He retrieved the letter he'd been given. "Bessie and Lily Bardill—"

"Georgia Bardill's twins?"

"That would be them. Since they're only five they had their babysitter write up a letter of recommendation for Sven Dante. Apparently he runs the snow plow around town."

"Okay." Roxanne laughed.

"They would like him to be part of the auction so a),"—he unfolded the letter and read it out loud—"their mom can have a Valentine and b), they want Sven to build them a snowman. I think there might be a song that goes with that."

"There is. How cute will that be? That gives you eight." She ran through the list of services again, from the accounting help, to furnace repairs, they had a pretty good selection of offerings—and bachelors to go along with it. "I have another stop I want to make later today. At this rate I'll hit fifteen before we know it."

"You're sounding pretty confident."

"I am. For the first time in a long time. It's pretty much killing me, but I'm trying to keep my excitement under control for a change."

Guilt suffocated the dread piling up inside of him. He should have told her the truth from the start. He never should have let her get her hooks into this dream of hers that he was going to be able to save her. Save her business.

"Let's go over these new scheduling plans I have for the auction." She flipped the pages in her folder. "I need to get the details finalized so we can run the programs and flyers at the printers. And then there's the decoration ideas for the gazebo. I'm even thinking we should advertise online, maybe get some media interest in how the town's coming together to save the library. The media loves a humanitarian story, right?"

"So I've heard." There was no convincing her, not when he didn't want to dim those stars shining in her eyes. But he was going to have to. Soon.

But not today.

❖

"Morning, Dad." Roxanne bounded down the stairs ready to face the day and, if her math skills were up to speed, add the last bachelor and service to her auction list. Fourteen. She'd hit fourteen late yesterday afternoon thanks to Millie Antwerp and her sister Betty, who decided that their nephew Bo needed some socializing about town. What better way to introduce a newcomer—and a talented mechanic to boot—to Christmas Town than to toss him straight into a fundraiser.

The call from her lawyer the other day should have devastated her. After all, it wasn't every day a woman learned the business she built from the ground up was going to have to close. Learning that her former partner Clementine had been apprehended with the police and that the District Attorney was preparing an entire litany of charges, she now had what she needed to stave off the vendors and clients. It would take liquidating the business and selling her condo in Los Angeles and finding a job to start paying back the money that was owed, but the lions at the gate had been fed for a while. Today was a new beginning. Her new beginning in Christmas Town. One that started with going out and making new contacts with various local businesses that might be in need of her organizing and event planning skills.

Roxanne bypassed the coffee machine and checked her purse for enough cash so she could stop at the Tea Pot. Gina Banning made the best scones and Roxanne's rumbling stomach was begging for one—or two, along with a very tall, very strong coffee.

"You're chipper this morning." Calvin Prescott folded his copy of the morning paper, set it aside, and struggled to his feet, crutches and all. "Haven't seen you this worked up in a long time."

"I'm about to win another bet with Tristan."

"Is that so?" Calvin's gaze slipped back to the paper on the table, a frown creasing his expanding brow. "I hope the poor guy knows it's coming. He's had his share of bad news lately. Don't you go gloating, now."

"No." She shook her head. "No gloating." It didn't hold the appeal it once did. "It was bad news about his father losing his pension. I wanted to talk to you about that, actually." She hadn't forgotten. Not exactly. "Tristan can't understand why they have to sell the house. As far as he knew the mortgage should have been paid off already, if not soon." When her father didn't respond, she pressed him. "Do you know something, Dad? Something Tristan should know?"

"Probably."

"Dad. I know Paul's your friend, but if Tristan can help."

"Helene had a health scare. Turned out to be nothing, but the two of them decided they wanted to stop talking about traveling and actually go somewhere. So they took a second mortgage out on the house. Then Paul lost his pension and Helene's retirement doesn't go very far, so…." Paul sighed. "It's been hard on them, but they're managing."

Roxanne's good mood deflated. "Tristan needs to know."

"Agreed." Calvin nodded.

"But if I tell him—"

"If you tell Tristan, Paul will know where he heard it. It's all right." He patted his hand. "Paul's a good friend. Sometimes you have to go against what they want if it's good for them. They don't want to leave Christmas Town. If Tristan can do something to prevent that, it's worth Paul being angry with me for betraying a confidence."

"You're a good man, Dad."

"Doesn't have anything to do with me. Paul and Helene deserve better than to be shipped off to Florida."

She agreed. The idea that Tristan's parents, who had always been so kind and welcoming to her, were going through such a terrible time broke her heart. "There must be something we can do. Can't someone talk to the bank? They've lived here forever, Dad. They're as much a part of Christmas Town as The Knotty Elves or Christmas Town Workshop or…they're supposed to live happily ever after. They kissed in the gazebo on Christmas Eve all those years ago."

"And they got married the following spring, just like the town legend says. There's no guaranteed happy ever afters for anyone, Roxanne. You and I know that better than most."

Roxanne nodded. She'd been just fourteen when her mother had died from ovarian cancer. From the time Shelly Prescott was diagnosed to the time she passed, they'd had four short months. Months Roxanne had spent promising her mother to excel in every way possible for the rest of her life. She'd managed to do that, professionally at least, for a time. But as far as the rest of her life?

"Helene was Mom's best friend," Roxanne whispered. "We can't let this happen."

"The Ramseys are proud, Roxanne." Her father made his way over and dropped a hand on her shoulder. "Don't make a big fuss over this. Everything will work out the way it's meant to."

"Yes, it will." She nodded. "You going to be okay today? I need to head into town."

"I'll be as fine as I was yesterday and the day before. Just a few more weeks and I can ditch these metal monstrosities. It'll be good to have you home full time, Roxanne, but don't go thinking you have to smother me with attention. You've got your own life to lead." He headed out of the kitchen, then stopped, looked over his shoulder. "You know, it's funny. There's this look you used to get, just around graduation time. This shiny, dreamy kind of look whenever you talked about Tristan. I didn't think much of it at the time, but I've seen it again since he's been back. I know you think you don't want what your mother and I had—"

"He's practically engaged, Dad." She flicked a quick, sad smile. "To a woman named Savanna Bond. So it doesn't matter what I want."

"Doesn't it? It's funny, isn't it? How life and this town, seem to give us exactly what we need. I see it every Christmas, with every couple kissing beneath the mistletoe in the gazebo. I think maybe it's time you stopped focusing on what you think you want and see what's right in front of you. You and Tristan both came back at the same time. There has to be a reason."

"Dad." Roxanne shook her head. There was a reason: the Knotty Elves. "That's not fair to him or Savanna."

"Just a bit of advice from an old man. Take it for what it is. Have a good day, honey."

"Yeah." Roxanne fiddled with a loose thread on the tablecloth. "You, too."

❖

A few short days before the auction, Tristan walked out of Dockery's Department store just as his phone went nuclear. Between the emails and text messages he didn't need to read a single one of them to know he'd been fired. The relief of it just being over surprised him. He'd been so worried about perception, about what people—his parents, the town, Roxanne—would think of him losing his high-priced, high-powered job, that he'd let that be the driving force of his obsession.

In the end, he'd been fired because he'd tried to do the right thing and if he was going to go out, that was the way to do it. The uncertainty of what was to come? He'd worry about that tomorrow. Or maybe the day after. He'd been fortunate in the salary he'd made, and had been careful. He'd be okay for a good while. Hopefully long enough to figure out exactly what he wanted to do from here on. Maybe he'd go to trade school. Take up carpentry or welding or, heck, maybe he'd go to Los Angeles and help a friend salvage her event planning business.

Roxanne.

His stomach sank like a stone. He'd run out of time. He had to tell her the truth. He could only hope that she'd understand why he hadn't told her before and that maybe, once the fog of his employment issues and his make-believe fiancée disappeared, Roxanne would be amenable to finding out what lay beyond a heart-thudding, mind-blowing kiss in the shed.

"Tristan!" A dark sedan pulled to a stop along Main Street, the window sliding down to reveal the familiar, friendly, and oddly welcome face. "Now that's just lucky. I'm getting out here, Pervis. If you could drop off my bags at the Pine Tree Inn, I'll manage on my own from here."

"Very good, ma'am."

"Savanna, what are you doing here?" He didn't give her a chance to answer before he wrapped her in a hug so tight, he was afraid he'd break her ribs. "Your father has to be going crazy about now. You should be with him."

Blue eyes glistening with sympathetic tears, Savanna tilted her head back to look at him. Sunshine and roses didn't have anything on Savanna Bond. "And that reaction right there is why I told my father

he's a complete idiot for firing you." She kissed him, a great big smack, on the mouth. "You did not deserve any of this, Tristan. Not one bit of it. He needs more agents like you, not fewer."

"They needed a fall guy." Tristan shrugged. "I understand that."

"That's the shock talking. And for the record I do not understand." She swept her cream-colored jacket behind her and tucked her arm securely through his. "You and I should go somewhere to talk. I have so much to tell you. But how about you show me some of this pretty little town of yours first? Where's that kissing gazebo you've told me so much about?"

❖

Ticking off the fifteenth box on her bachelor list didn't bring her the excitement and happiness Roxanne hoped for. She was grateful to Grayling MacIver, the new owner of the Pine Tree, for volunteering her vacationing step-brother and his professional chef skills to the cause. As a former record executive, Grayling had some experience cajoling reluctant participants to moving outside their comfort zone. Clearly her immediate family was not immune to her persuasive charms. Giovanni Renzo hadn't stood a chance and, with a shocked nod and uncertain smile, offered his personal cooking services for up to a family of six for a month. Ca-ching!

Had Roxanne not been feeling a bit bogged down by her father's revelations about Tristan's parents earlier this morning, she might have done a very public and very awkward cartwheel right in the middle of Main Street.

She tucked her phone and notes away, heading down the street toward the center of town. She'd be early for lunch, and surprise Tristan. That would give her enough time to figure out how to tell him what he should know about his parents' situation.

Across the street from Dockery's Department Store she stopped, catching sight of Tristan emerging. She shivered, chills erupting along her spine that had nothing to do with the weather. Reaching up on her toes, she started to wave, but a long, dark sedan pulled to a stop in front of Tristan, blocking her view.

Even from behind, she recognized the elegantly dressed blond who emerged from the back of the car. But it wasn't the way she threw her arms around

Tristan, or the way Tristan embraced her. It was the solid, familiar kiss Savanna Bond placed on his mouth that caused an odd sinking sensation in Roxanne's stomach.

The smile on Tristan's face, the absolute happiness she hadn't been able to pull out of him in the past couple of weeks, broke something inside of her. She couldn't move as she watched Tristan and Savana move off down the street toward the town square. How could this have happened? She rubbed a hand against the center of her chest, willing her heart to start beating again. She'd fallen in love with him. But when? That day in the shed? Sitting across from him at Posey's drinking a strawberry shake? Bantering over the bachelors in town they each hoped to procure for the town auction? Or…had it happened….

Tears burned the back of her throat. Or had it happened all those years ago, on a beautiful, early summer night, when she'd dared to kiss the boy who had always been there.

When more than a few people stumbled around her, she mumbled an apology and moved out of the way, stepping back against the building and tried to decide where to go. Tried to decide where she belonged.

"Nothing's changed," she whispered and swiped at the few tears that escaped her control. "Nothing's changed for him. This is all you, so pull it together. He's your friend, remember. You want him to be happy." And clearly Savanna made him happy. She needed to embrace that, if only for a few more days. He'd be leaving soon. With Savanna. He'd be starting a new phase of his life while Roxanne would come home, to Christmas Town, and start her own.

Alone and without Tristan.

"I feel like I've stepped into a postcard, everything's just so gorgeous." Savanna plopped onto the bench next to Tristan, a box of freshly popped popcorn in her hands. "Has popcorn ever smelled so good?" She stuck her nose in the container and inhaled. "I've missed carbs so much."

"Well, if you want a good dose, we'll get you to Posey's. You can't miss there."

Savanna shifted on the bench and faced him, crossed her legs. "How is it you seem almost happy at having been fired?"

"Not sure I can explain it." He'd had time to get used to it and, somehow, even after receiving the call from the Vice President of the agency, he realized the anticipation had been far worse than the reality. "I was miserable as an agent, Savanna. Everything's so superficial, so financially motivated. So cutthroat. I don't think I realized how miserable I was until I came back here."

"You were a great agent," she corrected. "But you were an even better friend."

"It's funny. Just when my parents are leaving, I'm thinking about coming home. Talk about being the king of bad timing."

"Nothing stopping you now. Oh, that reminds me." She pushed her popcorn at him and dug into her purse. "I wanted to deliver this in person. Or rather, I told my father I'd deliver it in person. Right after I told him about me and Eddie."

"You finally told him?" Tristan wasn't sure who he was happier for, himself or Savanna. "How did your dad take you falling for the head of agency security?"

"Considering he and everyone thought I was about to marry you, he was definitely shocked. I'm sorry it took me so long to figure things out. You've been a total sweetheart playing pretend until I got my head together. It's hard, giving up the expectations people have for you, especially when your heart goes somewhere completely unexpected."

"I take it you've finally talked to Eddie?"

"I have. He's meeting me up here for Valentine's Day." Savanna took back her popcorn and began to eat again. "It took some doing, convincing him that I was ready to be a real grown up and stand up to my father. What happened with you helped me do that. Here." She handed him a thin envelope. "It's the least you deserve and honestly, I think you should ask for more, but I know you. You won't."

"What is it?" He flipped open the edge and pulled out the check. The very significant, generous, and quite unexpected check. "I don't understand."

"I suggested you deserved a stipend for throwing yourself on the publicity pyre. You were the one who found out about the company's illegal production policy. You tried to warn my father, you tried to warn everyone. It was their fault they didn't listen to you so." She shrugged. "That should give you a nice cushion until you decide what to do next. Is that actually a shop that sells socks and gloves? How cute is that?" She shifted around as Tristan clearly wasn't paying attention. "Oh, hello."

"Hi."

Tristan's head snapped up at the sound of Roxanne's voice. "Hey. Oh, hey, yeah. Roxanne, great. Good timing. This is—"

"Savanna Bond. Yes, I know." Roxanne stepped forward and held out her hand. "It's a pleasure to meet you."

"And you." Savanna stood up. "I was just admiring this darling little town of yours. Tristan's always spoken so highly of it; I couldn't wait to see it."

"It's a good place to come from," Roxanne said. "I, um, saw you two headed this way and thought I'd introduce myself. Just as a friendly welcome," she added, adding another surprise to Tristan's already overloaded day. "I'm sure you two are going to be busy planning your wedding and all, but in case I didn't see you again, Tristan."

"Of course we're going to see each—"

"Can we?" She indicated she wanted to speak with him alone. "This will just take a minute," she added to Savanna.

"Not a problem."

"So." She cleared her throat when they were by themselves. "I talked to my dad this morning. About your parents. Since they didn't tell you, I'm sure they don't want you to know or to worry, but just before your dad lost his pension, he took out a second mortgage on the house. They wanted to do some traveling. Instead…." she cringed. "That's why they're moving."

"I knew it. I knew there was something else to the story." He slipped his hand around hers. "Thank you for asking. And for telling me."

"Dad and I agreed you needed to know."

"I appreciate that."

"I got the fifteenth."

"The fifteenth?" For a moment, he didn't understand. Then he remembered. "You won the bet. Okay, you had your confession time, now it's mine. There's something—"

"I'm not going to collect."

"You aren't?" He should have felt relieved. He didn't.

"You were right. It was never fair. I was going to win either way and I don't want to save my business by forcing you to turn over your client list. Especially when now there's no business to save."

"Why not?"

"Long story." She tugged her hand free and waved away his concern. "You have other things to focus on now. I'm going to go back and close everything out, pay off who and what I can, then make arrangements to do more once I get a new job. Here. In Christmas Town."

"You're coming home?" Hope ballooned inside of him. "For good?"

"It's where the heart heals best, isn't it? I'm going to look into some jobs, see what there might be for a former professional event planner."

"Anyone would be lucky to have you. But about the bet—"

"It's done. We both know I goaded you into it in the first place. You never could say no to me." She smiled and leaned over, looking at Savanna. "He's a great guy, Savanna. The best friend anyone could ever have. I'm sure you know that already, but… yeah." Her lips curved in a quick smile. "I hope you two will be very happy together."

Tristan reached out for her, but she was too quick. Roxanne hurried away, hands shoved deep in her pockets, her chin tucked into her chest.

"That's her, isn't it?" Savanna walked up beside him, wrapped her arms around Tristan's and squeezed.

"That's who?"

"The one who got away." She smiled up at him then bent to retrieve her purse and popcorn. She stepped away, heading toward The Pine Tree Inn. "I always suspected you had one. You'd best go after her, Tristan. Before she gets away again."

The day before Valentine's Day, Roxanne sat in hers and Tristan's booth at Posey's, going through her checklist one last time. The flyers for the event had been printed and distributed around town. The schedule of events had been created and sent to all interested parties, along with being sent to the printers for distribution.

Boxes and Boughs were on board to help with the decorations at the gazebo, which was just enough for them considering the expanding family situation of the local event company's owners. They were looking to cut back some and, after a few conversations, Roxanne had agreed to come on as their new business and on-site manager. She had also talked to Marnie Collins up at Bells Are Ringing Wedding chapel about one of their openings, so as far as employment was concerned, she was going to be fine.

She'd head back to Los Angeles in a couple of weeks, close everything out, put her house on the market. And then she'd come home.

As proud as she was about taking charge of her life and situation, she was equally as ashamed at the lengths she'd been going in order to avoid Tristan and Savanna. She'd definitely heard the gossip about town, and how thrilled everyone was with the socialite. Tristan's fiancée was indeed one of the rare women who managed to exceed expectations.

Tristan, on the other hand, had managed to surprise her. She'd read it online first, less than an hour after she'd seen him in the town square with Savanna. Since then she'd heard various versions at various town hot spots for gossip. That Tristan hadn't told her about his troubles at work disappointed her. Not because he hadn't trusted her. Well, not exactly. Most of her disappointment came from the realization that she hadn't made him feel as if he could. Looking back, she could see where he'd tried, but being single-minded individual she tended to be, she hadn't been paying attention. She wanted to be there for him, but he didn't need her. She had no doubt he'd come through it all just fine.

She hoped he'd be happy. As much as she was capable of hoping these days. Self-pity wasn't her default position by any means. She'd get over him. Move past it. She'd be okay, too. Eventually.

"Mind if I join you?"

Roxanne stared as Savanna Bond slid into the booth across from her. Gone was the designer dress and pricy shoes and jacket she'd been wearing the other day at the town square. With her hair braided, and the bright yellow t-shirt and jeans, the socialite looked as if she'd taken a very long, very relaxing vacation.

"Tristan said you're addicted to Posey's strawberry shakes."

"I, um, yes." She glanced at her half empty glass. "Guilty as charged."

"Great. The perfect recommendation." She signaled to Posey, who waved back and nodded. "I've become a bit of a regular, I'm afraid. Good thing the Pine Tree put in a gym, otherwise I'd gain ten pounds in this town."

Roxanne flashed a smile. "How are you enjoying Christmas Town?"

"It's fabulous." Savanna reached out for a fry, hesitated to ask permission, and Roxanne nodded. "I'm thinking it's the perfect location for a low-key wedding. Just a few friends, close family. Give them a bit of sightseeing interspersed with the nuptial events."

Roxanne nodded, feeling slightly sick. She liked Savanna. She liked her a lot, but talking about her wedding to Tristan might just cause irreparable harm to her own heart. "Christmas Town excels at weddings. I could give you some recommendations if you'd like." She dug into her purse for the brochures she now carried.

"Actually, I was hoping you'd agree to be my wedding planner." Savanna pulled Roxanne's forgotten plate closer. "Okay, these are crazy good. What the heck. Thanks, Posey." Savanna smiled as her milkshake arrived. "I'm going to have to start sleeping on that treadmill. So what do you say?"

"I-I'm flattered you'd think of me," Roxanne admitted. What she wouldn't have given to hear this offer weeks ago. "But I'm sorry. I don't think I'm the right person for the job. You and Tristan—"

"Me and Tristan?" Savanna snorted and had to grab a napkin. "You mean he still hasn't told you? Oh, Roxanne. I'm so sorry. No. I'm not marrying Tristan. He's a friend. A good friend who pretended to be dating me until I got my head out of my butt and realized how much I loved someone else. He really hasn't told you?"

Anticipation built inside of her. "I've been kind of avoiding him. And you. Both of you."

"Well, Jiminy Christmas, he just dropped a few notches on my perfection meter. Men. Okay, in his defense," she grabbed more fries and drank more shake, "he's been busy dealing with his parents and the bank, paying off that mortgage of theirs. He's also sending them on a three-week cruise in Europe. He's going to unpack the house while they're gone."

"They aren't moving?" Had she kept her head buried so deep for so long she'd missed everything going on in town?

"Nope. They're staying put. And, I'm pretty sure they aren't the only ones. Tristan's planning on sticking around, too. You meant it when you told him you were going to move back, right?"

"Yes." Was it possible…?

"Well, then, I'd say you need to talk to someone about all this, don't you? If only you knew where he…ah. Wonderful timing as ever. Hey, handsome." Savanna beamed up at Tristan as he approached the booth.

"I have been looking everywhere for you." He slid in beside Roxanne. "You're hiding from me."

"I was, yes." She tucked her hair behind her ear. "I thought…that you two…." She glared up at him. "You lied to me. About a lot of things."

"Not exactly." Now he plucked up a fry and grinned over at Savanna. "You assumed, based on your vast Internet explorations that we were a couple. I just didn't deny it. That said, I couldn't very well marry someone when I've been in love with you for most of my life. Oh, there's my backup plan now. Ladies." He stood up and greeted Odette, Prudence, and—looking as spry and healthy as ever—Ms. Baxter. "An empty booth right here for you so you can eavesdrop without straining yourselves. I need as many witnesses to this as I can get."

"Witnesses to what?" It was only then Roxanne realized how quiet the diner had become. "What's going on?"

"What do you think?" Ms. Baxter remained standing behind Tristan as he dropped to one knee. "Boy's been planning this since the two of you were scrambling around the jungle gym."

"That's so cute." Savanna leaned her chin on her hand. "I love a happily ever after."

"So do I." Tristan reached into his pocket and pulled out a ring, a thin gold band, small triangular diamond surrounded by half a dozen smaller ones. "I know this is kind of sudden and we've got a few long conversations ahead of us, but I want you to know what I'm thinking. And where I hope we're heading."

Roxanne blinked down at the ring. He didn't need to hope. The second she saw him walk into the diner she knew what she wanted her future to be.

"It was my grandmother's. My mom hadn't packed it yet, so I took it as a sign. I know it's not that big—"

Roxanne sobbed. She slapped both hands over her mouth to stop herself, but she couldn't. The tears exploded in her eyes as she stuck out her hand. "It's beautiful."

"I'm not entirely sure what the future holds. I'm still exploring my options."

"We'll figure it out." She pushed her finger forward and knew, as the ring slipped into place, she'd never take it off. "We'll figure all of it out. I love you." She clasped his face between her hands and kissed him. "I think I've always loved you."

"She's the only one who didn't know it," Ms. Baxter chided as the diner erupted in applause. "If we can get these two together, we can manage anyone." She nodded firmly to her friends before joining them in the booth. "Now we want to hear all about the auction and just how many bachelors you've got lined up."

"In a second," Tristan murmured against Roxanne's lips. "I think we might just pull all this off. Auction, wedding. Marriage. Kids. The whole thing."

"You want to bet?" She laughed, her heart light in her chest.

"On you?" He stroked a finger down her cheek. "Every time."

Copyright © 2019 by Anna J. Stewart.

Sharon Stevens is a proud mother of three amazing young men, grandmother to three beautiful girls, a MA Creative Writing student and a primary school teacher for nineteen years. She has been writing for some time, with several pieces of work in print and online venues and has self-publish her own book. In her spare time, she looks after her granddaughters, cooks, reads, writes, knits and spends time with family and friends. Her passion is to write, and she is making every effort to transition from being a primary school teacher into writing. Over the years she has supported many community projects and still continues to do so today.

HAPPY ANNIVERSARY

by Sharon Stevens

"Are you ready yet, Jen!" growled Charlie. "We need to get to the airport by six, and it's already two-thirty!"

Jen and Charles were going away on a cruise to celebrate their twenty-fifth wedding anniversary, "…but lord knows why?" was the thought that went through Jen's head.

It had been Charles's idea, but she couldn't fathom his intentions. After all, they weren't really communicating. She was buried in her job, looking after the children while looking after her mother too. He was buried in his career, his sport and his friends. They seemed not to have much time for each other.

The children had already been shipped off to their aunts and uncles for the two weeks that they were going to spend at sea, island hopping and soaking up the sun. Jen was given the task of telling the children:

"You two, come and sit down, I've got something to tell you."

"You're getting a divorced," they chorused together. "Come on mum, we could see this coming. The atmosphere…" they continued, "and when you speak, you only end up arguing!"

"No, not at all!" Jen retorted quickly. Then, "Is that what you think, really?" She looked in the faces of her children.

The children just looked at each other as if there really was no point in replying. The evidence of their parent's relationship—or *lack* of relationship—spoke for itself and it appeared Jen and Charles hadn't done enough to hide it.

"I'm sorry. I didn't want this for you…" Jen continued sadly.

So, surprisingly to Jen and Charles, the children had been excited by the fact that their parents were going away and they will be spending time with their cousins. It was not the reaction. "We've decided to go away for a bit, just the two of us. Your dad, he surprised me." She did not quite expect the reaction she got; they cheered!

" I know, I'm gonna bring my guitar and docking stations. I'm sure aunt Kaylie won't mind. In fact, Uncle Steve can help me learn some new tunes. Great!"

"I think that I will bring my iPad and some books. Aunt Kaylie is great at trying out new hairstyle too. Mia's hair always looks great."

Jen was disappointed. She couldn't help but think that maybe it was because recently "home" hadn't been too homely and welcoming with her and her husband hardly speaking. When they did talk, they only barked at each other. Jen and Charles, in an attempt to protect the children, clearly failed at pretending they were a happy family.

"I don't think that we're proving anything to them," Jen confessed to Charles later that night.

"What do you mean?" Charles replied, annoyed. He made it plain he was doing his best, and the problem was "her." She's never happy with anything he did—that's what he told his friends. Jen had found out from one of the wives.

Jen, on the other hand, felt that it was definitely Charles' fault. He was never at home and when he was the conversation was about the game he'd seen with his friends, or he'd snap without listening to her requests.

"Don't tell me that you haven't finished packing yet?" Charles continued. "We're running out of time. If we don't hit the motorway by three 'o clock, the road will be chock-o-block! And I've got to load the luggage into the car yet!" Charles added urgently, more to himself because he knew that Jen wasn't really listening.

"I'm doing my best. There's just so much to do!" came the reply from Jen. "Just get the luggage into the car and I will lock the doors."

"What on earth have you packed—the kitchen sink? We're only away for two weeks and there is a laundry on board," came the even more angry response from Charles.

They travelled up the motorway to the airport as they always did, in total silence. To their amazement, they managed to get to the airport on time, because the motorway wasn't as busy as they had expected it to be. Exchanging the odd word now and again they boarded the airplane and found their seats.

"Why are we doing this, Charles?" Jen asked under her breath, not wanting the other passengers to hear.

"Doing what? Going on a cruise?" Charles whispered.

"No, not that. I've always wanted to go on a cruise. Why are we trying?" she said directly in his ear that time.

"Well, because..." Charles frowned. The long pause made it clear to Jen he didn't have an explanation either.

"You don't even know why? Charming! Typical. You, doing something without thinking it through! What a surprise." Jen had muttered louder than she'd meant to. Passengers nearby turned and looked at them both. She felt hot with embarrassment.

Stuck on the plane with her husband for too many hours to count, Jen stewed in her bitter thoughts. Charles had booked the cruise without telling her. It was a surprise—a surprise she could now do well without. How could he do this? He had booked it last minute, which meant that she'd had a hundred and one things to do before their departure, not including packing for two weeks away from home. And as usual, Charles didn't help with the chores at home. It was not his role, being the man of the house. Blah, blah, blah!

"Would you knock it off?"

She turned to see Charles was looking down at her hand, which she was anxiously and repeatedly tapping on the arm rest between their seats.

She grimaced and pulled her hand off the arm rest, all but recoiling from his words, from him. If

only she'd known he was like this before she had agreed to marry him, but she had been younger then. Just a mere young woman who was flattered that a man was interested in her. Plus, she'd had an imperative to do anything to leave home. She'd brought this life upon herself.

If only.... If only what? she thought. If only she could turn back the clock? If only she could go back and talk to her younger self? If only she had parents she could tell her deepest secrets and worries too? If only...what? Whatever "it" was, it was too late now; twenty-five years too late.

So here she was, on an airplane, travelling to a beautiful part of the world on a two-week cruise with a man she hardly knew now. A man who barely spoke to her. A man who had his own life. The life they'd once shared was the one that involved children now almost grown, and here she was in a confined space heading towards "alone time" together where they couldn't be distracted by things other than themselves. She was dreading it.

Charles glanced over at his wife, unable to hide his annoyance at her twitches of anxiety, fully aware his abrasive attitude had frayed both of their nerves. He had booked the trip on a whim. He'd been at the pub with friends from work, they'd had too much drink, and each had been talking about their marriages. Charles had mentioned that his anniversary was coming up and one of the guys had suggested a cruise to celebrate it, because it was cheaper than full-blown party.

He shook his head, noticing Jen's side glance his way. What a cheapskate he really was. Charles had sworn his friends to secrecy; he couldn't let Jen know....

Suddenly conscious of how far they had strayed from each other, Charles turned to face Jen. Looking into her eyes, he spoke steadily but nervously. "I want us to try, to try to see if we can make this work." He paused, then continued, more vulnerable. "We weren't always like this. We used to laugh and joke. We used to enjoy life and being with each other..." His words trailed off; he looked away.

Jen was surprised by his frankness but pleased that he had been honest. She wasn't aware that he was remotely bothered that things had changed between them; he hadn't shown it before.

"Ok then. I know we've not really been close for a while, but…I'm willing to try if you are," Jen said, feeling awkward with this display of affection in the close confines of a very public plane. She'd grown used to the way things were. Why change things now?

He reached across the space between them and picked up Jen's hand which was now plucking nervously at her pants seam. "Deal."

Resolutely, they both decided to try to see what this holiday might do to save their marriage.

Landing at Montego Bay gave them a chance to soak up some energizing sun before embarking on the first leg of their journey at sea. They made the effort to make some "small talk" which at times became tiresome, even while relaxing on a sun lounger side by side. Jen would glance at her magazine and then her book, not really paying attention to the words; Charles was not really listening to music on his iPhone, either. All they knew was that neither really wanted to be there.

On the first evening on board—after the staff tried to sell the many excursions, beauty treatments and the many top ups that were available—they went reluctantly back to their room to change for dinner. Since it wasn't the meal with the captain, they dressed smart but casual. Jen made an effort to put some makeup on (something she did only for special occasions); Charles wore a colored shirt and white linen trousers.

She could tell Charles had forgotten how to be patient—polite, even. It no longer came naturally to either of them. But he shifted from foot to foot while she was getting ready, then he complimented Jen for the first time in a long while. She surprised herself by returning the compliment, something that she hadn't done either for a very long time.

Jen had thought that Charles looked handsome, his sun-kissed skin shining under his open-necked shirt. Charles noticed that Jen looked attractive in her bright Ashanti cloth dress. Both felt slightly less uneasy to be in each other's company.

At the table, they met other couples; who were celebrating different milestones in their own lives; this included a retired couple that still looked very much in love. Jen and Charles became very interested in them, both wondering, "How did they do it?", to be in love after being together for the length of time that they had. They were envious.

After the meal they decided to go for a stroll around the ship, not wanting to join the others at the disco. They'd both felt pressured to play a role that neither of them wanted to—or rather, knew how to play anymore. The expectation that they were happily celebrating twenty-five years of marriage was too much for them to act upon, when they had only shared strained words for years at home.

It was Jen who broke the silence first, as they passed yet another couple having a stroll and taking in the fresh sea air. "I wonder what's their secret?" Jen queried, fanning herself.

While wiping sweat away from his brow, her husband responded. "Hmmm, you've read my mind. I was thinking the same thing too."

"I might just ask Mavis—that lovely woman we just had dinner alongside—if I get chance at breakfast," Jen responded, ever hopeful that Mavis' and Walter's relationship might help theirs.

After being at sea for two full days, trying to keep busy on the ship and their relationship afloat, they finally arrived at their first destination: The Dominican Republic. They spent a day visiting the main tourist areas, such as Santa Domingo, La Romani and Punta Cana. Charliesand Jen found it easy focusing outside of their marriage to spend time studying the historical artifacts and buildings they encountered in their travels. This was the one thing they always had in common and could enjoy without any pressure.

They'd also spoken to Mavis and Walter and had asked about their secret to keeping their marriage alive.

Mavis looked at her husband, her love in her eyes. "You need patience."

"Aye," Walter responded, his smile gentle and full. "And perseverance."

Mavis laughed. "Oh, yes. And the ability to realize that it is all not candlelit dinners and roses. Life gets hard."

Walter nodded. "You doubt yourself and your decisions. You doubt each other."

Mavis reached forward and traced an elderly hand down her husband's cheek, cupping his jaw. "But then, at some point, you realize that no matter how much he gets on your nerves, your life would be so much harder if you had to go through all its hurdles alone. You realize your love is worth the effort."

"Everything worth having takes work," Walter confirmed, leaning in to kiss his wife with as much tenderness as the first time, despite the Parkinson's shaking his frame.

One of the things that they'd recommended was finding common ground, something that interested both parties, so they were trying.

Later they travelled to Puerto Rico, St Thomas, St Maarten, St Barts, St Kitts and Nevis, Antigua, followed by Barbados, Curacao and Aruba, then back to Montego Bay. They soaked up the sun, dipped their toes in crystal clear seas, and ate succulent fruit freshly picked from trees laden with bounty. They danced to local music, visited colorful galleries, toured museums full of ancient artefacts telling a story of past events, all surrounded by brightly colored picket fences, people with dark shiny smiley faces selling their wears to the visitors intruding on their islands.

"Oh, I loved the jelly coconut in St Maarten, I've never tried anything like it." Jen mused. "I can see why coconut water has now become so popular; that was delicious and so cheap!"

"Yes, it was tasty, but I loved that Bajun flying fish with cou-cou. I could eat that again. I wonder if we can get that at home?" Charles recalled, licking his lips as his mind took him back to the restaurant they'd visited.

The barriers that Jen and Charles had built up around themselves—*between* each other—over the years slowly began to crumble as they found themselves talking about, and showing an interest in, the local histories of the places they visited. They realized that sharing their pleasures increased them ten-fold. They even joined in the late-night events on board ship, dancing late into the night or gambling at the casino. They even dressed formally for dinner at the Captain's table.

One of the other passengers at the table had noticed a change in their demeanor from their very first meal on board the ship. "Someone got some last night," the woman said as she bumped her elbow to Jen's.

"Sir, madam—can you look directly into the camera please?" a photographer interrupted. "Sir, can you place your left arm around her waist, like so…."

The photographer's words encouraged Charles to put his arm around Jen in public and he got a thrill when Jen reacted as if it was a thing they did every day. She moved her body to fit into the arch of his arm and pushed her herself into his side. They looked comfortable and smiled as the camera clicked to capture the change in their behavior; a welcome souvenir of their trip.

Holding hands was also something they'd not done since just after their second child had been born. Yet Charles attentively took Jen's hand and led her to the dance floor for the last dance of their cruise. She melted in his arms.

"I love you," whispered Jen, wrapping one arm around Charles' waist and raising a hand to cup his face in a gesture not unlike Mavis'.

"I love you too," responded Charlie, kissing the top of Jen's head, holding her tightly in his arms. He didn't want to let her go and in their room that night, for the first time in too long, they became one in a way that they both knew was the beginning of something new in their marriage. Not back to "how it was," but something better…stronger. They now knew they could weather any turbulent seas—as long as they did it together.

Copyright © 2019 by Sharon Stevens.

Kathryn Kelly writes sweet contemporary romances, historical romances set mostly during the American Civil War and the antebellum south of Louisiana. These are the stories of southern belles who find love amidst the turmoil going on around them. In addition to writing about the present and the past, she also writes time-travel romances, merging yesterday with today, believing we find our soul mates no matter where—or when—we have to go to find them. To learn more, go to www.kathrynkelly.com and sign up for her newsletter. She lives in Louisiana.

BLUE AND GRAY

by Kathryn Kelly

CHAPTER ONE

Natchez, Mississippi
October 1863

Mary Montgomery stood in front of a flyer tacked on the outside wall of the General Store. The piece of paper, whipped by the early morning wind, was the only one left. Usually there were at least half a dozen flyers posted on the wall.

She shivered and tucked her hands in her dark green velvet shawl. Her long winter dress was normally warm enough for the mild Natchez, Mississippi winters, but this day was particularly blustery. She took a step forward when a horse and wagon rumbled behind her. She looked over her shoulder, recognized the driver, and waved.

"Morning, Miss Mary," he called out as he slowed.

"Good morning."

"Everything as good as it can be?"

Mary smiled. "Under the circumstances, yes."

The driver nodded and continued on his way.

She savored the little piece of hard candy Mr. Nate, who owned the hardware store, had given her. It was almost impossible to afford any treats these days if they could even be found, but since she was five years old, coming into the store with her father, Mr. Nate always had something for her. Sometimes it was a piece of candy, sometimes a little ribbon for her hair, or even a piece of leftover cloth at the end of a bundle. Those were her favorites. She'd made several quilts out of them.

Lately, though, no one was buying material, so remnants were few and far between. It was all about survival now with the war putting a stop to getting much of anything brought in. There were the blockade runners, of course, but Mary couldn't afford their wares even if she tried.

Things had been going well until her father took ill. First his hands began to tremble until he could no longer write legibly. After that, he began having trouble getting around. With less and less nutritious food to eat, he declined further and was currently abed.

Mary's father was a bank officer, but since his illness, and with the war going on, Mary was struggling to take care of the two of them. Her mother had died in giving birth to her—her parents' first and only child—so Mary felt quite alone in the world.

Fortunately, she had friends. Her best friend was Sophia. Sophia's mother had died last year, and her father was fighting in the war, leaving Sophia to raise her two younger siblings.

The two girls, Mary and Sophia, relied on each other for support more and more.

Mary read the flyer again. She'd heard there was a Yankee hospital set up in one of the abandoned plantation houses just outside of town. Here was evidence, if ever she'd doubted it.

According to the flyer, the Yankees were looking for women to work as nurses. *No experience needed*, which suited Mary just fine. She had no experience as a nurse. Well, except for taking care of her father, but that was a different a kind of care. Certainly not the kind of care an injured soldier would need.

Her first instinct was to dismiss the whole idea, but one line snagged her attention. *Payment issued in the form of ham and fresh biscuits.*

They certainly knew their audience. The residents of Natchez, like most of the south, were starving. Any opportunity to get food had to be considered.

Not just for her, but for her friend, Sophia, who was taking care of an eleven-year-old girl and a seven-year-old boy. The boy, Caleb, had Mary's heart. If she had food left over after feeding herself and her father, she'd give it to her friends.

The flyer said travel papers were needed. Mary was friends with the Lieutenant over at the home guard. Getting papers for the two of them would be easy enough.

It couldn't hurt anything to at least check the offer out. The flyer said a wagon would pick the girls up in town tomorrow morning.

She took a deep breath, thought about her father. He always told her not to let opportunities pass by. She would have to get travel papers for them, convince Sophia to go with her, and make sure her best dress was in good shape.

She decided to go by the home guard first. That way Sophia couldn't use that as an excuse.

Both of them needed the food.

Even if they had to put their pride aside and work with the enemy.

CHAPTER TWO

There was no reason to be nervous. Mary stood in the Yankee hospital and waited her turn to check in.

It didn't smell like a hospital. In fact, it smelled good. She'd detected a scent of vanilla and cinnamon when they walked in the front door. Now as she and Sophia waited in what looked to be a man's study, she distinctly smelled tobacco.

Good tobacco.

Her father had entertained enough over the years for Mary to know good tobacco when she smelled it.

Something felt wrong. She hadn't seen a single injured man. And why were the girls being called up one by one?

"Next," the man behind the desk called. His foul mood was obvious in his tone.

Two women have already been assigned to different men and escorted out of the room by a young soldier, barely old enough to shave. When Sophia's turn came, the man behind the desk had personally escorted her…somewhere, then he came back and, with the same foul mood, gestured for Mary to approach his desk.

She hesitated. Every instinct she had screamed at her to run.

But she couldn't leave her friend, Sophia, here alone with these soldiers. She was the one who'd convinced her to come in the first place.

After giving the man her name and address, she, too, was escorted from the room by the young sol-

dier. He led her into the foyer, then up the stairway. Again, she saw no injured men. In fact, all the men looked healthy and the three men they passed by looked at her with obvious curiosity and more interest than she would have liked.

He knocked on one of the rooms and opened the door.

Mary turned away, suddenly apprehensive.

"Wait. Miss. You'll like Gabe."

Mary turned back. She couldn't leave anyway. The wagon that had brought them into town didn't leave again until four o'clock. So, she—and Sophia—had all day here, whether they wanted to stay or not.

This soldier, the one escorting her to the one named Gabe, was friendly enough. Perhaps if she met Gabe, she could find out what was going on here. It occurred to her then that these could be injured officers who needed individual care. They would naturally have been separated from the enlisted men and given special treatment. The thought made perfect sense.

The young soldier opened the door and Mary stepped over the threshold with renewed confidence. The door closed behind her.

The soldier, Gabe, stood up and met her just inside the doorway.

Gabe was a tall man—a least six feet tall—and he was older—around thirty. He was a handsome man with a heavy stubble. His eyes were deep blue, and his full lips had a kind smile. He was wearing dark blue trousers and a white shirt. No jacket. He didn't appear to have any injuries.

Mary returned his smile, but hers held questions.

"May I take your cloak?" he asked.

"Oh." She'd forgotten that she was wearing a cloak. "Please." She shrugged out of her cloak and handed it to him. He laid it across his arm and gestured with his other hand for her to sit.

"There aren't that many options," he said, his tone apologetic. "But I thought the table would serve us best."

"Of course." Mary sat in one of the two chairs at the tables. She had no idea how the table would be of use. There was an empty vase on it and a daisy lay on the table.

"Would you like a glass of wine?" he asked, standing a few feet away.

"Oh, no. Thank you." Mary was taught that southern ladies didn't drink alcohol. Up north, though, it might be different. She had a distant cousin who lived in Pennsylvania who, according to rumor, drank alcohol on a daily basis.

"My apologies. Would you like some tea?"

Tea. He had tea. Mary hadn't had tea in at least a year. She felt her eyes light up.

He grinned. "Tea it is then."

While he made tea, Mary looked around his room. It was a sitting room adjacent to a bedroom. She could see the bed through the open door. The bed was neatly made and from what she could see, clothes were neatly folded in the open wardrobe.

Her mouth salivated at the lovely scent of mint tea. It had been her favorite, but they had been out for so long. First, they'd tried sassafras root, then blackberry leaves, but finally Mary had given tea up completely. If she couldn't have real tea, she would do without.

He set the glass of tea in front of her and she closed her eyes as she tasted that first sip. She took another sip. Then opened her eyes. He was sitting across from her, his eyes trained on her face.

Her skin flushed at his appraisal. "It's been so long since I had tea."

"I feel like I should apologize for that."

"Why would you ap—?" She stopped herself. He would apologize for being the enemy. For his contribution to the southerners' lack of food and drink.

"I didn't want to take part in this war," he said. "But as a doctor, I felt I should try and help those who did fight."

Relief washed over her. Gabe was a doctor. Of course. They'd been assigned to various doctors then. "They didn't tell me you were a doctor."

"Ah." He waved a hand. "It didn't seem important."

She squinted at him. How could it possibly not be important? "I don't understand."

"This is unrelated."

"But your patients…"

"I don't have any patients at the moment. Of course, if I'm here in case I'm needed."

"Then what do you do?"

"Paperwork. I order supplies for the doctors in the field."

"That sounds like an important job."

He nodded. "Someone has to do it. I admit it wasn't my first choice."

That explained why the man at the downstairs desk asked if she could read and write before assigning them to various soldiers. "You need help with your paperwork then."

He looked at sideways. "Not really."

"What then? Someone to make you tea and such? I can do that."

He laughed. "There's no need for you to do that. I can make you tea."

"Are there injured soldiers then?"

"Not here."

"I don't understand. The flyer said you need people to help with nursing injured soldiers."

A look of understanding crossed his features. "You're here to volunteer for nursing."

"Yes. I mean, it said we'd get ham and fresh biscuits."

"I think it's actually bread and potatoes and maybe some beans, too."

Mary's eyes widened. So much food. But for doing what? "I'm so confused."

"I believe there were two advertisements. One was for nursing care and one was for…companionship."

"Companion—" Mary put a hand over her mouth as she tried to make sense of what he was saying.

"Some of the men were lonely. They have no one to talk to. No females. So, our commander thought this might be a positive way for them to pass the time."

Mary bit her lip. *I will not panic.* "But I thought I was going to a hospital. To nurse soldiers." Oh my. This was not at all what she expected.

"It's a type of nursing, I suppose," he said with a small smile.

Mary had, of course, heard about the prostitutes Under the Hill, down by the docks. It was considered the unsavory part of Natchez. A lady would never go there. It wasn't proper.

She straightened her back and clasped her hands tightly in her lap. She'd made a mistake in coming here. She wasn't sure how it had happened, but it had. "My friend and I aren't companions."

"No. No," he said quickly. "Truly the men just want someone to talk to."

Mary pushed back her chair and stood up.

"Please. Mary." Gabe stood up also. He looked so much like a lost puppy that Mary just froze, looking into his eyes.

"You're here. Just give me a little of your time."

He was right. She was here. And if she left here, she would be alone. Alone among these men. These Yankee soldiers. The thought was somewhat distressing.

She melted back into her chair and picked up her glass of tea. She drank deeply. Besides, he had tea.

"Thank you," he said softly. "I can only imagine how foreign it must be for you to be here."

"The whole war has been foreign. After a while it seems that foreign becomes natural."

His lips curved into a smile. "It does, doesn't it?" He slid the daisy toward her. "This is yours if you want it."

She picked up the flower and slid it into the vase.

He smiled, picked up her empty glass, and took it with him to the little cabinet where he kept drinks. He refilled her glass with tea, handed it to her, and filled another glass with whiskey.

Sitting across from her again, he took a sip of his whiskey. "Mary Montgomery," he said. "Tell me something about you. About your life."

Mary didn't mind talking to people. And she'd never minded talking about herself. But she'd never told a Yankee soldier anything personal about herself. What could he possibly find interesting about her? "I'm not sure what you'd like to know."

"I don't care. Anything. Did you grow up in Natchez? Do you have a husband? Children? What do you enjoy?"

Mary raised an eyebrow in amusement, still cautious. "Yes. No. No. Not much of anything these days."

"Do you have family?"

"My father." A flash of guilt followed. She hadn't even thought about her father since she'd arrived at this house.

"Does he know you're here?"

Mary shook her head. "Heavens no. Besides—he's not well."

"What's wrong with him?"

"He's lost most of his strength. It's gotten worse now that we have very little to eat. It's gotten so bad he's abed right now."

"I'm sorry to hear that."

"Since he's not able to work anymore, I have to do what I can to provide food for us."

"I see. That's why you answered the advertisement."

"Exactly." Mary realized that she was relaxing in his company. This was the opposite of the way it was supposed to go.

But the men weren't the only ones who were lonely during this war. Mary had many acquaintances that she spoke to regularly. And she spent time with Sophia and her young siblings, but it had been so long since she'd actually sat and had a conversation with a man. She hardly knew what to say.

CHAPTER THREE

Four hours later, Mary sat on one end of Gabe's sofa and he sat on the other. They'd talked all morning and through a lunch of fried ham, potatoes, and biscuits. Mary couldn't remember the last time she'd eaten so well.

How the Yankees got food when the southerners couldn't was baffling. But she didn't dare ask too many questions.

The sun was streaming in through the window now and she heard the soldiers going through their formations.

She glanced at the little clock on the end table. It was three hours before the wagon was scheduled to leave to take them back to town.

Mary wanted the time to slow down. She wasn't ready to go back to reality.

The reality of not having enough food for herself and her father. Sure, they would give her a bag of food as payment for the day, but it wouldn't last forever.

The reality of taking care of her father. Today a neighbor was sitting with him, feeding him. Making sure he stayed in bed and didn't wander off.

The reality of not having a man to talk with. Someone to actually converse with.

She'd learned that Gabe was from New York. Not the city, but what he called upstate. He'd grown up in a small town, much like Natchez.

His father was a doctor, but he'd had no interest in the war; he was older and wanted to live out his days in peace. He had five siblings—two sisters. And he was the middle child. Gabe had been engaged to a young lady, but she'd died two years before the war started. Gabe hadn't said how she died, and Mary didn't ask.

He'd had said he had no interest in courting anyone since his fiancé's death.

He'd told her that the most profound thing he'd ever done was to go up in a hot air balloon. If flying was an option, and he could choose it over medicine, he'd do so without hesitation.

"I'm afraid that I don't have experiences that compare to flying over the trees."

"In some ways, I'm glad," he said. "Perhaps someday some lucky man will have the opportunity to share those things with you."

"You have an interesting way of looking at things, Sir."

"Please. You have to call me Gabe."

The war had changed things. All the rules were turned upside down. Here, she had spent the day with a man alone in what was essentially a bedroom, and no one would raise an eyebrow. Possibly because she wouldn't go around telling it, but still, before the war, a lady never would have risked her reputation this way.

And a lady never would have given her time in order to be paid in food.

Yes. Times were different.

And Mary was certain that things would never be the same again.

At a quarter to four, Mary told Gabe that she must leave.

"I know you have to go," he said, then a little more quietly, "but I wish you could stay."

Mary smiled, but she felt a sadness inside. That was the thing about breeding. It was indelible. As a southern lady, she would never show strong emotion no matter how strongly she felt it.

When he held out his hand, she placed hers in his. He kissed her knuckles. "May I see you again?" he asked.

"I don't know." She glanced at the clock again. She couldn't allow the wagon to leave without her. She had no other way home.

A man called out from below. "Last call for the ladies heading back to town."

"I'm sorry." She pulled her hands from his. "I have to go." She picked up her skirts and darted into the hallway, down the stairway, and out the front door.

Seated next to Sophia on the long ride home, Mary was silent.

Her head was filled with Gabe.

Heavens.

She had a crush on a Yankee soldier.

CHAPTER FOUR

Two years later

Mary went to the cupboard, took out a basket of fresh beans, tomatoes, two bright red apples, and set them on the dining room table.

At least once a week, sometimes two, for the past two years, a bag had been left on her front doorstep during the night. There was no particular night—it could be any night of the week. She'd tried waiting up a few times to try to catch who it was, but she never did spot them.

She considered that maybe it was improper for her to accept it, but she had better sense than to starve simply because of a little pride.

The bags had started coming after she'd met Gabe. She had to leave her address when applying for what she had believed to be a nursing position. He had to be the one having them delivered. There was no other explanation.

She thought often and fondly about the day they'd spent together. She still thought about him and wondered if he was well.

She wondered if he'd gone back to New York.

She had given some thought to looking for him, but she couldn't figure out how to go about it. Only a couple weeks after that day, she had heard that the Union soldiers had pulled out.

It was baffling where anyone could find that much food. It certainly wasn't readily available to anyone Mary knew. And it wasn't just food. One time there had been ten yards of light blue cotton material in the bag with the food. She'd made it into two lovely everyday dresses. Another time there had been candles. And soap.

But most importantly, the regular delivery of food had been life-changing.

Her father appeared in the doorway. "Good morning."

"Good morning." Her face brightened at the sight of her father. Since he'd been getting regular nutritious food, he'd steadily improved. He hadn't gone back to work at the bank yet, but they were both optimistic that he would be well enough soon.

He picked up an apple and bit into it. Mary silently thanked Gabe, just as she had hundreds of time before. Even if he hadn't been the one to send the bags of food, she gave him credit.

He father sat at the table. "I'm expecting Johnathan Jones to stop by today."

"He answered you about the job, then?" Her father had been hesitant to ask about returning to work, but she'd encouraged him to at least make an inquiry.

"Yes. I forgot to tell you about the message that came yesterday."

Mary had spent the day at her friend Sophia's house. Mary and her father weren't the only ones who'd benefited from the gifts on her doorstep. Sophia and the children also had regular nutritious food.

Someone knocked on their front door. "That must be him now," Mary said, heading toward the front door.

"He said he was coming this afternoon," her father acknowledged, but she shrugged it off. People had been known to change their minds.

She opened the door without looking outside first. "My father is in the kit—" She blinked. It was him.

It was Gabe.

He was wearing black civilian pants and a matching jacket. But she recognized the grin that had been seared into her memory. He handed her a white daisy.

Propriety be damned. She threw her arms around him.

He picked her up and twirled her in a circle.

Mary's eyes filled with tears. Out of a devastating war that had created a rift in their country, love had been kindled out of the compassion between two people who were supposed to be enemies.

North and South.

Blue and gray.

Copyright © 2019 by Kathryn Kelly.

Rei Rosenquist is a queer agender (they/them) speculative and contemporary fiction writer who depicts a wide variety of identities struggling to find a place in a wide variety of worlds. They are also a lifelong barista, baker, and nomad. Over the years, they have traveled to many countries, engaged many peoples, picked up new habits, and learned new languages. But some things never change. For them, the constants of life are made up of love stories, great coffee, delicious food, and seeing the world. Rei's work can be found in previous Heart's Kiss *issues,* Enter the Aftermath *by TANSTAAFL Press, and* Summer Sizzles *by Fiction River. You can find more of Rei's work by visiting their website at reirosenquist.com. Stay in touch via Facebook (Rei Rosenquist), Instagram (@rylrosenquist) and Twitter (@rylrosenquist).*

TABLE FOR TWO

by Rei Rosenquist

There's a specific table in the corner of an upper room in a building in Portland, Oregon.

The type of table doesn't matter. It can be tall or short, round or square. It can have four legs or three or a central pedestal. It can be made of real wood, fake wood, glass, plastic—whatever you like. It needn't even be a table, specifically. Could be a rug, a pillow, a cushion, or simply a circle of well-arranged stones.

It's a place where people gather, that's what matters.

Likewise, the upper room can be in any sort of building. The business or body inhabiting the space can be any business, any body. Even the corner itself need not be a corner, specifically. It could be the edge of a round room. It could be the single last standing two-by-four in a pile of rubble.

Regardless, it will always be there—this table in this corner of this one upper room. No matter what happens to humanity, to cities, to the notions of tables and buildings with upper rooms.

Why?

It's a permanent gateway to a dimensional rift.

Dr. Jo Marble, my mentoring professor, published the research exposing the gateway two years ago. The rift exists as a timeless rip between this reality and what Marble calls "outspace." In the multiverse, that's where all energy comes from. The Zeroth Dimension. The blank space between everything and nothing where anything can be whatever it likes.

I was shaken by her discovery, and it quickly became the root of my doctoral dissertation in astrophysical quantum mechanics.

My hypothesis was that whatever lived on the other side of the rift wanted to communicate *something* with humanity. I decided, due to the strangeness of the research, it would best if I collected all my own data first hand.

Dr. Marble warned me against this.

"You'll have to show evidence that you've safeguarded the data against your own lens," she said ten months ago in her oak and black chiffon office.

"I'm not a very prejudiced person," I said confidently.

Dr. Marble sighed. "I know you'd like to believe that about yourself, Fig. We all would."

"You know who my parents were," I defended.

My parents had been active members of the QUILTBAG community, as well as activists for the polyamory community. If anyone was able to do this research, it ought to be their son. We'd gone back and forth for an hour, and finally Marble caved.

"I'm going to trust you, Fig. Don't let me down."

Over the next ten months, I became that one weird customer every shop must have. The quiet eccentric regular who orders the same tea every day and sits in the same chair for ten to twelve hours and works silently at a laptop.

Today is Tuesday, and the rain-drenched streets of the city are pretty much empty. A gray sky hangs low and heavy with clouds as I lock my bike under a blooming cherry tree. Pink petals mingle with the rain, falling all around me. The air is cool and sweet with their fragrance.

Despite the sunless sky, these flowers always remind me of brighter times.

I sigh, heavy with nostalgia and longing for a younger me who used to believe in the limitlessness of life's possibilities. Then, things changed. My parents died, I went away to college with no one by my side. I moved into the guy's dorm, and I made friends who talked a lot about politics and sports. We rarely shared how we felt about anything personal. We definitely didn't talk about our families. And we didn't cry about the past.

Among my new friends, I've tried to stay true to the Fig inside, the Fig my parents could have been proud of. But sometimes, I couldn't always remember where I once drew those lines. And I got lost in pop culture, in ideas that weren't mine.

But, in the tea shop, doing my research, I feel grounded. My project is the one good thing I have in life. My safety net.

I push open the door that leads into the tea shop stairwell and climb the two flights quickly, with a researcher's haste, eager to get lost in my work. Once in the shop, the smell of tea wraps me up like a warm hug. I let the age-worn wooden door fall shut behind me, breathing in deep.

Behind the glossy dark wood counter, I see the familiar face of the weekday manager.

She's older than the rest of the crew. I've always placed her right around my age.

She wears only floral print dresses that compliment her woodsy brown skin. She has one pair of work shoes, and they are these impressively big, chunky, black knee-high boots.

It's a look. A good one.

Her hair is a lopsided, house-made shave on one side, long feathered hair down to her elbows on the other. The long portion is always a new shade of the rainbow, never the same from week to week. I admire the amount of dedication such hair must take.

She wears a pin on her shoulder that says "She/Her/Hers thnx" right next to a big blue, pink, and white trans flag patch. The patch is hand-sewn on with gold floss and each stitch is perfectly executed.

She works way too much, and her name is Petunia. Today's floral gown is a magnificent slim-line silken white dress full of huge red and black poppies. It flows around the ankle of her black boots like a river as she swirls onto a stool to take my order.

"Morning-o!" I say with a little too much enthusiasm, cringing at my own voice.

Petunia jumps, startled by my loud greeting. "Oh, Fig. It's you. Hi."

Perfect. I've been here for less than five minutes, and already I'm acting like one of those obnoxious loud-mouth guys on my hall, like I think the whole world must be happy to see me. I pick up a tea menu, despite not needing it, and turn the pages to avoid making eye contact. I don't want Petunia to think I'm annoyed by her lack of enthusiasm. I honestly don't think she needs to be pleased as punch to serve me. I should be honored she even remembers my name.

"Vanilla Rose Chai. Big pot, please," I say, making an effort to speak softer than before.

Petunia nods.

I always order the vanilla rose chai in a big pot.

The smell reminds me of my childhood, of a happier version of my life. Where my three parents are still alive. Vanilla and rose were their collective favorite smells. Everything in the kitchen and bathroom drawers was always some variation on the theme.

Psychologists say that our sense of smell is most closely linked to nostalgia. Breathing in the tea shop's vanilla rose chai isn't just like sticking my nose into the past, it's like swinging open a door and walking in, sitting down at the dining room table and watching my parents smile across triangular tea sandwiches at me.

I wish, every day, they were still here.

Petunia bobs her head and takes my card without another word. I appreciate the silence as I leave the tea counter, my heart heavier than usual.

It's not just the memory of my parents that hurts today. It's also because I'm so close to the end of my research. By the end of the day, I will likely have the last three to five samples I need to write my completed dissertation.

The end of the project also means the end of my long days in the tea shop. I'll miss this place. It's become a part of me in ways I'm not sure I understand. Significant for its realness. Like a light shining on a high hill in the long stretching valley of my isolated academic life. This place has somehow filled up a gaping hole inside me, even if only momentarily.

My therapist, Dr. Harmon, would have a lot to say about that, I bet.

But still—I love this spot and my place in it.

Petunia brings my tea over and I take it silently, nodding thanks. She disappears behind the tea counter with a swoosh of silk, and I pull up my laptop and open my spreadsheets.

The first shift is uneventful, and I sip my tea thinking less about the project and more about what I'm going to do once I've finished my dissertation. I've thought about applying to teaching positions around the country, take a year off to travel and see

the world, or go in for more research and start applying for astrophysics teams looking for a doctor of dimensional quantum flux.

Nothing's resonated yet.

But, Dr. Marble gave me two years. The fact I've done the work in ten months is almost obscene. So, I have time to formulate a more complete life plan. Fourteen months, to be exact.

Still, I think about the future sometimes and I worry.

Dr. Harmon might say it has something to do with my parents' death.

Learned fear of the end of things.

The door of the tea shop opens, and I lean forward expecting my first couple of the day. Instead, it's one of the weekend crew coming in to say hi. I bob my head at them, since we're now looking at one another, and across the room, I see Petunia come into view. She gives me a look that I find unreadable.

I wave because now I feel extremely awkward, and she waves back stiffly, looking perplexed.

Good one, Fig.

I sink back into my laptop, cheeks burning, minding my own business—which, at this point, is doing nothing but trying to look busy while I wait for a couple to fill the chairs of the table across from me.

I can still feel Petunia's eyes on me, but I do my best to look occupied by making notes to myself along the lines of, "Don't be a fucking creeper, Fig!" and so forth.

The thing is. Petunia pays me more mind than any of the tea shop's weekend crew. I've thought on it quite a bit. Talked it over with Dr. Harmon. We've concluded the added attention is wariness. Most likely my lack of social skills in combo with my steady presence in the corner has been misinterpreted as flirting.

I'm definitely not flirting.

Petunia is cool and interesting, but I'm not looking for anything like that.

It'd be complicated.

To start, I have what Dr. Harmon calls "emotional baggage" from my parents.

Not because my parents were strict or judgmental or anything like that. I was the lucky few who had parents who were gentle and kind, loving and careful, and they helped me figure out what the road to my future looked like together. Granted there were three of them and that made some social situations more...awkward. But to no fault of theirs. They did all they could to make sure I lived a well-adjusted life with a toolbox full of coping mechanisms and ways to express myself.

They were the best.

But, they're all three dead now.

Plane crash from Portland, Oregon bound for Los Angeles, where my parents were flying in to attend my undergraduate graduation ceremony. It was one of those ridiculously short flights that no one ever thinks will go down. 767s and 747s flying over the ocean go down. Everyone dies. Little prop jobs from one West Coast city to another don't crash.

They just don't.

Until they do.

Dr. Harmon reassures me that it's going to be okay, but maybe I should take it slow on new emotional connections for a while.

I went against her advice straight away. Jumped headlong into a relationship with a very smart, very cool post-grad genetics TA named Julie. Needless to say, things went poorly.

We had one huge blowout fight. Not exactly about my parents, but sparked by a comment I made about what a great example they'd set for me. We were at the park having a black bean burger BBQ, and Julie threw hers on the plate so hard it came apart into ugly brown and black bits.

She gave me this *look*—eyebrows in a tight line, lips puckered up like she was going to spit. A long breath hissed from her lips and she said, "Fig, you're delusional. All that queer shit and polyamory garbage is the collective disease plaguing the Earth!"

I thought to respond with something clever like: "Not, y'know, pollution and human greed?"

But instead, I said: "Then, I guess you can't love me."

She got up. "I don't think we can be together. I thought you were one of us."

She never explained who "us" was, but I knew. She meant cis-hetero folks. But, I was cis-hetero. And, I didn't like the feeling of being accused of being queer. It felt like an attack, and it hurt. I knew my parents would be disappointed in me for feeling how I felt, but I couldn't remember why.

So, I asked Dr. Harmon for advice.

She suggested I spend some time in self-exploration. She recommended books on identity. She reiterated the fact that maybe romantic entanglement wasn't quite the right thing for my personal growth right now.

"Being queer isn't a black and white line, Fig. You can be queer and be lots of things," she said.

"But, I'm not," I'd argued. "And I don't like people accusing me of things."

I'd stopped talking, stunned by how right she was, shocked I'd been saying it without even noticing. Like being queer was a crime, and I'd been judged without being given a chance to prove my innocence.

Dr. Harmon looked at my twisted up face and softened her tone. "Give yourself time to just be," she suggested.

That's what I've loved about these ten months in the tea shop. There, working on my project, I got to just be. Me. Whoever that was. No labels and no identity. There, I'm just Fig, the weird customer.

This is exactly what I need.

So, no, I'm not flirting with Petunia.

I finish off my big pot of tea which has long since gone cold now. I head up to the counter to get round two.

As I head toward the counter, Petunia is sitting on a stool reading the latest *Tea Professionals* magazine. Bathed in the warm overhead lighting, her face is full of soft angles and warm shadows I've never noticed before. Like a map unfolding, her beauty unfurls before me. When her eyes meet mine, I look away automatically. My hands tremble slightly as I deposit my dishes in the bus bin and make my way back to the register. I pick up a menu, trying to avoid further eye contact so I don't look like a creepo .

"Well?"

I look up, and Petunia is staring right at me. Her eyes are deep pools of dark intensity, two massive gravity wells of dying stars.

I can feel my face going warm, so I bury my nose into the menu I don't need.

"Uh, a, um, the—"

"Your usual?" Petunia says, no doubt to help move me along.

My second drink of the session is always a hot matcha with honey.

Petunia makes the best matcha in the city. No question.

I look up and accidentally get pulled into Petunia's gaze. It's the first time I notice how eerily similar to mine her eyes are. Almost like looking into a mirror at a more compelling, more interesting, more diverse version of myself. I blink and the illusion is gone, but then I realize Petunia is still waiting for my response. I nod, trying to smile and feel like I'm flinching.

My fucking stars, this is going downhill quicker than usual.

"Err, yeah, thanks," I mumble, embarrassed.

Petunia takes my card and smiles a lopsided grin, looking both amused and confused.

I can feel myself starting to blush.

The tea shop door opens and in strolls a guy in a baseball cap and a girl in ripped jeans and a crop top. I'm not surprised when they make their way to the table in the corner before looking at menus.

My saving grace.

"Back to work," I mutter an excuse to dart away from the counter as soon as Petunia hands my card back.

She gives me a look I can't read along with my credit card, and I worry I've been creepy or rude. I take my card quickly, leave a generous tip, and dash back to the safety of my laptop. Time to get to work. Something I can handle. Hours of intense focus. Allowing myself to just be. Fig, the silent observer. Fig, the five-senses and a scientific mind—nothing more.

The couple gets up to make their order and comes back over to the table, settling in for their date.

To the unknowing eye, the table looks like any old second-hand cheap wooden table. It looks faded and warped, but it's mostly the fake wood veneer peeling away from what is actually pretty decent wood underneath. The chairs, too, appear to be big box store rip offs of real vintage velvet-covered chairs, complete with crimson artificially-stressed velvet that's gone a rosy pink. But upon extended examination, I've realized they're actually vintage and the velvet is the real deal. So are the crusty oxidized copper divots holding the fabric down.

They sit in the usual configuration: guy on the right, gal on the left, the corner nearest me between them. Perfect for viewing.

I make note of physical descriptors for both of them. I call him Blue and her Red.

They're both fresh-faced, definitely college-aged. Most likely new to the area. Based on the number of layers, I'd say down south, maybe California. Both are Caucasian, pale as the inside of bananas.

She's got freckles and red hair. He's got brown hair and blue eyes. They're both dressed in exactly what you'd expect. She's in a loose black dress with leggings. Her poofy coat is olive with a faux fur hood. He's in a charcoal gray V-neck, brand name zip-up hoodie, and a matching wool greatcoat.

Their hands are both neatly folded around their steaming mugs of tea. I can smell the cinnamon and black pepper from here. Ah, Kashmiri. A good choice. Something sweet but a little sharp and spicy; something to get the blood flowing.

I make a note.

They're talking about dating, as all the table couples do.

She's been seeing a few people but she's not that into them.

He's been single for a couple months now, and he's ready to commit to something.

Their hands shift from their steaming mugs spilling the scent of Indian spices into their nostrils. Their fingers touch, tentative. She smiles. He winks.

All this as I'd predict, based on the last ten months of watching couples.

I make more notes.

As they get up and leave, I watch them pause and gaze into each other's eyes. A silence opens between them that from the observers stand-point is awkward and strange. To them, it's probably all butterflies and mush. She smiles again. He winks back.

They take each other's hands and leave the shop, just like every couple who sits at the table.

It doesn't matter how incompatible their conversations are. They always leave together, hand-in-hand, making googly eyes at one another.

I make my final notes.

Petunia sweeps through the cafe and wipes down all the tables. She pauses by the table in the corner, wiping it with a special kind of care. It's funny. I've never noticed her give that table much attention. In fact, I have no memory of her ever wiping it, resetting the chairs, relighting the candle.

Obviously, she regularly does these things. It's her job to make sure each table is ready for the next customers. And, Petunia does her job with passion and a careful touch. She wouldn't neglect a table just because it was in the corner.

So, why do I have no memory of it?

The question is a crack in a pane of glass inside of me. A small piece slides free, and a hole opens up inside of me. And in that hole grows a worry.

What else haven't I bothered to see?

I scan my document in front of me.

For the first time in ten months, I'm struck by the fact that all my notes look suspiciously the same. Every couple I've noted at the table is "standard cis-male" and "standard cis-female." Not a single queer couple. No non-binary individuals, no trans men or women, no genderqueers. Not a single "they/them/their" with even a question mark on any line. Not a single note that reads: "Identity & sexuality: I'm honestly not sure."

Under conversations, I see scattered but identical remarks. "Guy talks politics" and "Gal talks about shoes," among other details that sound like a bunch of cis-hetero clichés in hindsight. More striking, though, is that I haven't written down a single "Gal talks about politics" or "Guy talks about shoes," or so on. Everything neat and tidy, divided evenly along the well-published cis-hetero lines of American pop culture.

That can't be real, can it?

Like Petunia tending the table in the corner, I've missed something obvious. Only, I can't see exactly what it is. I feel like I'm trying to catch my reflection in a dirty mirror. There's all these tiny gaps and pieces missing. I'm about to go back through my document, trying to figure it out, when I'm caught by the sound of the tea shop door opening and closing.

I fully anticipate my next couple. A chance to prove myself.

Instead, my eyes are greeted with bright red poppies on a white silk background. Petunia, who left sometime while I was focused on my couple, has returned with an armful of shopping bags. She meets my eyes and nods. I smile without meaning to.

"That looks heavy. Here, let me get that for you," I say, offering to help.

"No thanks," she says with a frown.

She effortlessly swoops into the shop, the three bags moving fluidly like an extension of her dress. I look down into my lap, flummoxed. But then, I remember our gender dynamic—me being cis-male and Petunia being trans. And, I can hear in my head things guys in the dorm say. Off-hand comments about how gals are just naturally weaker than guys. Snide comments about how trans gals like to act like they're weak too so they can "pass" as real gals.

My stomach drops, and I feel awful for the offense I may have caused.

"I don't think you look weak," I say without thinking to Petunia's back.

I hear a slight gasp of surprise, which makes me decide to keep speaking despite how awkward this scene now is. "And I don't think I'm stronger than you…. You're perfectly wonderful and capable."

My comments are, however, not perfectly socially acceptable in public, and a few of the patrons at other tables chuckle or whisper.

From the counter, though, Petunia actually gives me a thumbs up.

And everything else disappears. The tea shop. The rift. My research. The whole goddamn multiverse. All that exists is Petunia and her being happy. The warmth in my chest is bright and surprising. And for the first time in ever, I know what people mean when they say, "my heart was glowing."

I feel certain I could light up the whole tea shop from the inside.

"Busy?" Petunia asks, eying the opened laptop in front of me.

I realize I've been staring. Not actually staring, more spacing out with my face and eyes pointed in the direction of Petunia. Which looks like staring. Goddammit.

"Yep. Lots to do," I mutter, my glowing heart crumbling back into awkward bits.

I quickly tuck back into my work without another word. I've filled up another two hundred rows of prime information after the last couple, and I need to start corroborating some of this data. Get to the root of why the table seems so outdated and…well, bigoted. Exclusionary. That's going to take focus. I reach into my messenger bag, pull out my smartphone, plug my in-ear headphones in and tuck in.

The first song that comes up is by a queer black woman named Janelle Monet, and the lyrics are all about the pink of our insides. It's sexy and not cis-hetero by any stretch. I smile as I stare at all my disconcerting data sheets. This is just the vibe I need.

I can't help but hear Dr. Harmon's voice in the back of my head, "Give yourself time to just be."

I scroll slowly through line after line of my data, being as present with it as I can.

Couple after couple have the same labels (made by me), and in my simplified notes, their behaviors all track with that data. But, then, an idea sparks in the back of my mind. And by the time I get to the last entry—"the Kashmiri Couple, Mid-Afternoon" I've labeled them—the spark idea has solidified into a distasteful concern. And, as I scroll back up to the top of my research, scanning as I go, that concern grows into a knot in my stomach.

Have I done just what Dr. Marble warned against? The very problem I was so certain I wouldn't fall into: observer bias.

I start looking more closely at the kinds of notes I've made. "Mentioned shoes" versus "showed off new shoes" versus "self-proclaimed shoe-fanatic" versus "likes functional shoes." In my mind, all of these cis-hetero gals had all "talked about shoes"—stereotypical female behavior. But there is a vast difference between calling oneself a shoe-fanatic (which ought to be open to all gender expressions) and mentioning shoes in a conversation with a relative stranger on a date to which one has probably walked (considering parking in the area is a joke). But, that difference is utterly unmarked in my research.

The answer is downright obvious now I'm looking at it.

I've let my anxiety affect my research. And what's worse, I've been acting like being queer is some kind of condition and I can use my science to prove I don't have it. At some point, I accidentally internalized the things guys in my dorm like to claim.

"*Being straight and, yknow, normal is just the way of nature, bro.*"

So, I went into this research already looking for cis-hetero clues that may or may not have been there. I interviewed no-one to cross reference. I didn't even expressly listen for pronoun usage or cues that someone might have been misgendered. I didn't note behavioral discomfort at potentially being mislabeled by a new date partner. I ignored all conversation topics that didn't fit the bill by deeming them "unrelated" or "undefined" and therefore not noteworthy. I just assumed.

I should be ashamed to call myself a doctoral student of anything.

Cenn, one of my three parents, once said to me, "Every person is like a building. Appearing like one cohesive thing on the outside, but truly made up of a complicated series of cluttered rooms on the inside."

Pear, the youngest of my parents would always add, "No person or relationship ever stands alone. Each one is a city intertwined with other cities stretching into the past and future forever."

And lastly, Mada would say, "But most importantly, Fig, don't get stuck in your own city's traffic jams and lose out on the infinite opportunities to go road-tripping into someone else's city."

Meaning, don't get boxed in by your own perspective and forget that nobody is simply what you see. A building's easy facade.

All these ten months, I'd done just that.

I'd leveled all the cities inside these people, gave them quippy labels, flattened them out into four tidy walls and slapped a banner on the building of their heart. All I'd seen were dresses and wool coats, sports hats and shoe obsessions. I hadn't once stopped and questioned my own assumptions or looked deeper than a few quick glances over the top of my laptop.

After ten months of research, I didn't know anything at all.

In the heat of my shame, I decide something:

I select the entirety of my research notes and I hit [delete]. I stare blankly at the flat white page. I save the empty document. I exit out of my word processor, shut down the laptop, and close the lid.

I lean back against the soft padded back of the armchair I've spent ten months sitting in.

It's all done. Gone.

I stare at the tea shop wall above my familiar table, blank faced and dejected.

What now?

"Fig? You okay, bub?"

I look up into Petunia's face, inches from mine. The soft smell of poppies wafts toward me. She has a way of doing that—matching perfume and dress pattern. Making herself a cohesive whole. I'm tempted to flatten her into a tidy building, too. To see only the one angle in front of me. Her sweet oak-colored face speckled as it was with faint gold dust.

But she is a city made of infinite interlocking streets.

All her complexities, her oddities, her struggles and her successes. Each significant moment of her life, an intersection lit with a dozen passing lights. It's like I'm looking through images of the Hubble Space Telescope for the first time. Glimpsing galaxies where my mind thinks mere stars ought to be.

The complexity, the breadth and depth of her being is immeasurable, and it's stunning.

My heart is pounding so hard at her proximity I can see my wire-rimmed glasses bobbing up and down with each thump. Tiny earthquakes of panic and regret.

"Fig?" she repeats, her voice taking on an edge.

I'm definitely being weird again.

"Sorry, I just..." I stall clumsily, having nothing to say.

What am I going to do? Tell her the truth?

What else do I have to lose?

I look up into Petunia's eyes and for the first time realized they were not just similar to mine—they were the exact same color as mine.

Cloudy sky blue with gold-brown flecks around the centers.

I blink, startled by sameness where I hadn't sought it.

"You look like you've seen a ghost?" Petunia says gently.

I don't say what I'm thinking—the bit about the vastness of her being. That would definitely sound like flirting. Instead, I say, "I just ruined my doctoral dissertation."

Petunia's eyes go wide. "You're working on a doctoral dissertation?"

I shrug—a determined effort to come unglued. "Was. Not anymore. It's a total loss."

"I knew it!" Her face is glowing.

"You did?" I balk, more than a little shook up.

She colors, her face going a deep earthy red. The color at the heart of a giant red cedar.

I try not to stare, and instead look down at my hands. They're the faded color of old bone. And they're trembling again.

"Not that you'd ruined it. No, I'm sorry, I mean that you were doing some kind of research. Working on a degree or something. Collegiate. You must be crazy smart.. Anyway, ugh. I'm rambling. I'm sorry. Can I take that?"

She gestures suddenly at my empty tea cup. Her other hand musses with the back of her hair, fidgeting. She's looking for an escape. I've freaked her out. I probably seem like a stalker or someone trying to impress her with some collegiate smarm. Mentioning my doctoral distress to show how smart I am. How much I outclass a tea shop manager.

Not the desired effect at all. So much for honesty.

"Sorry, yes please," I say, trying not to sound interested.

Or interesting for that matter. I just want to disappear.

She cocks her head at me, eying the mug that is still tightly gripped between my two hands.

I set it down so we don't have to touch hands. Her arm grazes my knuckles as she reaches for it. I feel myself blush, then wince, wishing I could hide under the table. Rather than look up and acknowledge the touch, I stare across my closed laptop at my sharp knees. The beige thrift store slacks I've got on remind me of the main character in *Death of Salesman*. The quintessential sad American man.

Then, her leg bumps into mine as she's headed back to the counter.

"I'm sorry," I mumble and try to shrink myself into the cushions.

Petunia—to my shock—chuckles softly. "Don't be. I bumped into you."

Left alone to brood, I open my laptop back up and login. As I wait for my desktop to load, I can hear Dr. Marble's voice echoing like a ghost in my mind.

You're always so careful. So attentive.

Only this time, I'd been careless. And sloppy.

I'd let myself down. Let Dr. Harmon and Marble and my own parents down.

If Petunia knew, she'd be disgusted with me.

About the only person who would be proud of the biased work I'd done would be my cis-hetero crusading ex, Julie.

Fuck me.

From around the corner, Petunia appears again with a mug of white tea. Peony. One of my favorites. "Made this by mistake," she informs me. "You want?"

I bite my lip, feeling bad. "I'd hate to take it from..." I don't even know who I'd be taking it from, but I feel bad, nonetheless.

Petunia smiles wide. "Okay, I'm lying. I made it for you. You look awful. How's it going?"

"Awful," I admit, then smile.

Petunia puts the tea down on my table and I breathe the soft florals in. Peonies and poppies—a perfect blend in my mind.

Petunia's face twists down into a frown. "So...what happened? Virus?"

I shake my head. "I deleted it."

Petunia nearly falls over. "What?! Why?!"

"Observer bias."

"Hm," Petunia hums and nods like she understands exactly what I mean.

"I have no idea what to do," I say absently, staring at the table in the corner. The one I've failed to understand.

"You ever sat there?" Petunia asks out of nowhere.

Before I can answer, the door of the tea shop opens. Petunia greets the customers with the typical "hey there" and a warm smile. I tell myself not to melt at that smile, but without the protective casing of my dissertation, I can hardly avoid the truth.

I melt like coconut oil in the tropics, stunned by her smooth, easy style. Her confidence. Her strength.

To distract myself, I turn to the couple and start taking notes.

At first glance, the couple is a cis-hetero gal and guy from a Hispanic background. They're speaking Spanish to one another and switching to English when speaking to Petunia. But then, Petunia responds in Spanish and that's the end of my understanding of the conversation.

So rather than eavesdrop, I start breaking down my initial biases.

The "gal," I noticed upon closer inspection stood in a wide, low-center-of-gravity stance not traditionally associated culturally with the female identity. "She" wore ripped jeans and a tank top, a gold bangle on "her" left wrist. Her shoes look like converse but have no label and the shoe laces are untied. Big hoop earrings weave in and out of her luxurious black curls that tumbled down her back and waved at me from across the room. "She" turned away from the counter and that's when I saw the very small pin on "her" shoulder. A yellow, black, white, and purple axolotl.

Non-binary.

The "guy" has one of those asymmetrical faux-hawk hairstyles with the long central strip of hair dyed to look like a peacock feather. "He" has several facial piercings, which accentuate the narrow mustache over "his" thin upper lip. "He" has on loose fit jeans, slim black leather-like shoes (could be vegan leather, I can't tell), and a blue- and gray-checkered neck tie that's untied and hanging like a necklace around "his" neck.

"He" is wearing a button-down underneath which is a floral print V-neck revealing the neckline of a sports bra or halter top or chest compressor. I can't tell which because I don't have experience with any of those garments of clothing.

I make note regarding my ignorance in this area as opposed to choosing a gender identity for this individual.

The two of them sit at the table across from me. "She" sits in the gal's position and "he" sits in the guy's position, and they share a pot of spiced chai tea. "She" talks about the supports in her rip-off brand shoes compared to "his" name brand Made in England Doc Martins. "He" talks about business practices connected to big name companies in countries like China. They discuss what first dates usually look like and how this is genuinely refreshing.

By now, I'd have put them down in the gal/shoes, guy/politics, and couple/dating categories.

I listen more closely, not writing anything down.

The one detail I would have gotten right is this: by the end, they talk about going and grabbing a drink, their hands cupped together. As "she" holds the door open for "him," their eyes meet, and I see the classic grin that I'd have recorded in my old spreadsheet as "date success."

The door closes, and the sound of heavy boots clop softly across the pale hardwood floor of the tea shop.

I looked up from my notes into Petunia's face.

"Well?" she asks as if we'd still been talking.

I glance at the time in the corner of my screen. It'd been forty-five minutes.

"Well what?" I ask, confused.

"Have you ever sat there?"

She points at the table.

A shiver of electricity sizzles down my spine and I squirm inadvertently.

"No, of course not."

"Then, how do you know anything about it?"

I blink. There's no way Petunia knows what I've been working on. No way at all.

"Why don't we try it out together?" Petunia holds her hand out toward me, offering me the chance of a lifetime.

I take her hand and follow her to the gateway of a dimensional rift. Her hand is warm and soft in mine. I don't ever want to let go. Petunia pulls out one of the antique faded-velvet chairs, and I sit in it.

The cushion is both softer and firmer than I'd expect. Across the warped table, Petunia pulls out the opposite chair and sits with her dress tumbling across her knees like a white, red, and black cascade.

I can just about hear water bubbling in the distance. A rolling brook, babbling sweet nothings in my ear.

And for a moment, I wish it was Petunia whispering secrets to me. The secrets of the universe.

What am I thinking?

"Close your eyes, Fig," Petunia's voice sounds bigger and deeper than it did before.

Like it's the ocean and my ears, a stony shore.

The sound is delightful, and I close my eyes without thinking.

"What do you see?" Petunia asks, voice echoing.

It isn't what I see that matters.

It's what I smell.

Vanilla and rose.

Not like the chai I'd been drinking, but something else. Something brighter and sugar sweet.

I know the smell in a flash.

It's the rose laundry soap Cenn used to use on all our bedsheets mingling with the sweet vanilla of Pear's sugar cookies. The sheets would be hanging to dry in the yard while the cookies cooled on the window sill. Work weary from the shop, Mada would swoop in just as the cookies cooled, slide them onto a big ceramic plate, brew a big pot of vanilla rooibos with fresh rose petals picked from the yard, and we'd all sit down around the big oak table and share dessert before bed.

It'd be Tuesday. Just like today.

And I'd be full of the feeling of community, connection, familiarity.

And most of all, love.

Deep down, like a light has been turned on, I know one thing to be truer than anything else in my life.

I want Petunia to be my community. Connection, familiarity and...dare I say it?

Love?

"Fig? You with me?" The massive gravity of Petunia's voice brings me back to the present.

I open my eyes and expect fully to see the tea shop again. Instead, I see a sky full of stars and galaxies.

Without having to ask, I know we've somehow tumbled into the dimensional rift itself. Sans table, sans corner, sans building, sans Earth.

I look for Petunia and see a bright light glowing gold beside me.

"Where are we?"

"Where do you think?"

"A tear in reality. A rift in dimensional space."

But how was I seeing it? How come others didn't fall into it like we did? Or...did they? Would I even know from the outside? What did customers sitting in the tea shop see now? Two cis-hetero-normative characters talking about dating and gently holding hands?

"But how? What's happening?" I ask, baffled.

Petunia grins wisely, like she knew I was going to ask this eventually and she's been waiting patiently for me to come around to the same reality.

"I opened the gateway up. I'm the guardian of this particular portal. And yes, my name's really Petunia. In case you were wondering."

What catches me off guard isn't "guardian," though maybe it should have been. It's also not that her name is really Petunia. Deep down I knew it was. Somehow.

No, what catches me off guard is the word "particular."

"There are others?" I muse. "More dimensional rifts? Here in Portland or spread across the globe? Do you guard more than one? Are there other guardians like yourself?"

I'm rambling, lost in ideas. Possibilities to reboot my dissertation. Ways to save myself and my career. If I could just see and compare multiple dimensional rifts, multiple tables in other corners of different upper rooms—maybe then, I'd come to a viable conclusion about the whole thing. Maybe, with more proof, I could understand.

There's a heavy silence between us, and I realize Petunia hasn't answered. I look through the strange darkness of outspace between us and I see Petunia's face, tight in a strange frown. Maybe it's the weirdness of the space, but all I can think is that she looks...disappointed. And sad.

Like she tried to offer me a present, and I threw it on the ground.

In a way, she did. She offered me her truth, and all I could think about was what I had to gain for myself.

Without over-thinking it, I decide to be honest.

"I'm sorry. I wasn't thinking. Or rather, I was. Of myself. My future. The dissertation. You're giving me a gift by inviting me into this space, and I've been ungrateful. Can you forgive me?"

"I forgive you," Petunia says, her face contorting in a way my human brain wanted to interpret as shocked. Only, I couldn't trust my human sensibilities here in the outspace. Could I?

Mada used to say I did that too much. Make assumptions, decisions involving others, project my will and desires onto the world around me. Of course, based on all my deleted research, Mada had been right.

I don't want to make that same mistake with Petunia. I want to get things right. Make her feel like the incredible cityscape she is.

Petunia looks away from me out at the millions of other galaxies, the millions of other places where—in the multiverse theory—we two could be right now. I'm glad I'm here with her now. Better than anywhere else I might be.

"Why do you think I brought you here?" Petunia asks quietly.

"To show me what I've missed."

"Look down."

I look at myself for the first time in outspace, and what I see is not the body of a man. It's not my body or any remnant piece of my perceived self-image. It's not even human, the shape of me. What I see is instead a small fire, burning yellow bright. In my depths I know what I'm looking at. My own personal shard of the star whose death birthed all life on Earth. The supernova that gave us the basic building blocks of DNA.

In an instant, all of Dr. Harmon's recommendations that I explore myself pales in comparison to the truth Petunia has shown me. The light at the very center of my being. I know beyond knowing that it isn't male or female. It isn't cis or trans. It isn't queer or hetero.

It isn't any label or any word I can even comprehend.

It is me without borders or barriers.

It is Fig. And, I am undefinable.

I look back to Petunia and find she is a bright gold fire flickering warmly across from me.

Massive and important. An undefined, undefinable city all her own.

And I know one thing.

We're great together. Uniquely balanced. Two stars falling into one another perpetually. Different and, yet, perfectly companionable.

White light flashes all around me like a screen reloading.

And in a mind-blurring whizz, I'm pulled back into the confines of 3-D reality.

I feel the vastness of myself folding up into my original human origami form. I come to and find we're sitting at a small warped table.

"Did you see?" she asks quietly, eyeing me.

I nod. "The rift is about connection—about seeing our true selves," I say, confident. "It shows you something you need to see—that it is only ignorance that keeps us apart, once you've found someone who fits you."

"Yes. Exactly. But, Fig—you should know. In this world, I'm not the same as you." Her voice is quiet, small. Full of nerves.

I smile wide. "I know. That's what's so great about you. I don't see a word or a label when I look at you."

"What do you see?" Petunia asks, careful now.

She's waiting for the other shoe to drop. Waiting with a guarded heart for all the bullshit things that cis-hetero-normative men say to wonderful, incredible trans women all the time. Things full of fear and hate I can't repeat. Projections of their own dysfunctions. I hesitate, unsure of my welcome, then put my arm across the table toward Petunia, reaching like I'm still a shard of starlight, hoping only to connect.

Petunia reaches back. Our hands touch. Skin against skin. Warm and soft. I'm sure I smell vanilla and rose weave between us. A dream of the past and a hope for the future.

I can hear Pear telling me "To be honest, always," so I go for it.

"I see someone I hardly know, but desperately want to. Someone who is a galaxy all her own. Someone who isn't a label or a type of identity. Someone I want to see more clearly, know more deeply every day."

This is definitely flirting.

Petunia colors, turns that soft red of a cedar's heart. And her eyes, so much like mine, dash away to the table and our touching hands. She's quiet, and I'm afraid I've said the wrong thing. And it's crazy, I know, but I have to let her know how I feel.

I take a deep breath. "You're someone I don't think I can afford to lose."

To my surprise, Petunia smiles wide and meets my eyes. "I've been feeling the same about you. When I saw you close your laptop, I thought for sure whatever your magnificent project was—it was done. And you were going to be gone. For good. I couldn't let that happen without at least trying to catch you."

"I'm glad you invited me to go through your gateway and meet you in the rift," I say, touching the edge of this table that is more than a table.

"I'm glad you said yes."

We lean across the table, our fingers entwined, and I'm surprised at how easily our lips come together, touching softly at first and then more hungrily. The vastness of her cities upon cities, galaxies upon galaxies, all spin together inside of me. And I know, this universe is so much bigger, so much vaster than I ever gave it credit for. The multiverse, more so.

I don't care about every other possibility out there. I care about this universe, right now, where Petunia and I are, together.

Petunia and I stand in unison like every other couple I observed. All those people that may or may not have been couples. People who fell into outspace together and came out holding hands. People who were or were not cis-hetero-normative, but who had assuredly made a connection by experiencing the expanse of the zeroth dimension and came out smiling.

Petunia waves at the counter that's been empty now for how long?

"Shop's closed. Want to grab a drink?"

"I'd love to. Can I help you shut things down?"

Petunia giggles in a way that's light and full of flowers. It's sweet, floral, and I breathe her voice in hungrily.

"Sure, grab a broom. You know how to sweep?"

I laugh and head in the direction she points me.

Sweeping is mindless and gives me time to think about what I'm going to say to my professor about the dissertation I deleted. Honesty is the best policy. I'll tell Marble straightaway that I messed it up. Observer bias. I failed. I'll start over. Base the initial theory on my own personal experience of the rift itself. Marble will be relieved I corrected the error before presenting. Maybe, she'll even be curious, and I can bring her to the tea shop corner and have Petunia show her the rift herself.

It'll take an extra year to finish my degree, but what's worth doing is worth doing well.

I finish sweeping as Petunia comes over with a red poppy-colored purse. She locks the shop and we walk away from the dimensional rift, hand in hand, like every other pairing who once sat there. Our eyes meet as she holds the door for me. My insides flutter like a bird springing from a tiny cage. Being in love like this is nothing like I'd ever expected it to be. Like Petunia herself, it is infinitely more.

A whole city to explore.

Petunia pulls me out from the tea shop, away from the puddles against the curb and out into a light rain. We dance out under the lights of empty streets. The air's coolness feels like a kiss from reality. She stops us in the middle of the deserted road while red and green traffic lights flash overhead. Smiling, she pulls me toward her. Our gravity spins us in a whirling circle, and our noses touch.

Petunia moves gracefully, her voice a breath in my ear, asking me for a kiss.

I offer up my mouth to her, and her lips are wet and warm against mine. And for a brief moment, the darkness of the saturated road and the lights flashing and spinning above our heads are galaxies that go on forever.

All those cities, all those dimensions, all those truths about ourselves are never really that far away. They're always right alongside us, waiting to peek out through the darkness and offer us a glimpse beyond the veil of reality where we are each the light of a unique star, and love is the gravity that draws us into each other's orbits.

Pamela Stewart's journey began a long time ago in a galaxy not too far away when the writing virus hit her in grade school. She has yet to recover. Two ornery cats call her mom, (two human daughters as well, but they may or may not claim her). She's a believer, a dreamer, a trier and loves superhero movies, driving cross country and unknown indie rock bands. She has an accounting degree that pays the bills but would much rather write. She placed third in the Rebecca Contest with her manuscript In Harm's Way *and won the Fab Five for* Frozen Hearts *(her best writing moment ever). If you like sci-fi and fantasy with humor, adventure, and a touch of romance, you'll love her stories. Her YA sci-fi series* The Ionia Chronicles *is about a girl and the android that loves her.*

DAMAGED

by Pamela Stewart

I fought through the dark water, searching for the surface. My sensors no longer registered which way was up. I didn't need air, but my human-modeled mind still sent a flood of panic through my nervous system.

Which was not helpful at all.

I suppressed the emotion as much as my processor would allow and assessed my dilemma. My short-term memory was compromised. I couldn't recall how I'd gotten in the water or what was happening. I did a quick scan of my systems. Most of my chassis was intact, although I detected massive feedback in my head from a blunt force trauma.

My logic circuit prioritized options. First, find the surface of the water. Second, determine the safety of the location. Third, reassess.

I never argued with my logic circuit in a dire situation. My emotional chip was on the same page. Get to the surface stat. My vision fritzed and scrambled. There wasn't enough illumination to perceive anything.

My body sank. With a chassis consisting of steel alloy, polyplastic, and flesh overlay, none of my parts were exactly buoyant. Though I didn't weigh much more than a human girl, I dropped like an anchor.

The trouble with being a companion droid used for combat included some major design issues.

I had the downloads and imprinting to swim but had never done so in a real situation. I stroked with my arms and legs, awkward at first, but then my programming hummed to life. Above me and to my left, a blaze of orange, red, and yellow flared through the water, and I picked up the muted audio of an explosion.

From the concussion and reverb, a medium-sized object had been destroyed, probably a marine vehicle. Fire equated to oxygen and that revealed the location of the surface. Using my backup hydraulics, I darted upward.

I broke the surface, my human-copied mannerisms told me to gulp in air. My flesh did need air to remain healthy, and it had been repressed for too long.

A body of seawater surrounded me in 360 degrees. Black sky met black water. The wind sprayed violent lashes of rain, and waves shifted my position. I fought to get my bearings.

A small boat sat five hundred meters away, glowing like a beacon. Fire reflected on the surface in long flickering ribbons of amber. I must have been aboard.

My scanners reached out but sputtered and failed. I had to rely on nearly human-level senses. It was maddening. No landmasses or seafaring vehicles appeared within visual range. What had happened to put me in this dire state?

I reviewed what I did recall. I was android Z12347, commonly known as Zee, a personal bodyguard for Kuta Cheng. I lived with him and his family on the mainland of NAR in the Xinjiang province. Flashes of our daily life scrolled through my memory. I reached out to the Cortex to see if I had a backup download of my memories, but my signal bounced back.

A three-meter-high wave pummeled me. Pain feedback rebounded in my head. My visual perception darkened.

To fall into standby mode spelled doom. I might be a non-organic life form, but I didn't want to cease to exist. The programmers had wired my body to experience a whole, unhelpful hodgepodge of human fear and anger and affection.

Fear won.

Where was Kuta? How would I save him if I couldn't save myself?

I would have traded all these super-not-useful emotions for a lifejacket or boat in the flicker of an impulse, but I didn't have a say in how my processor worked. I just managed my reactions.

I battled the currents toward the boat. If Kuta had been aboard, most likely he would be in the water nearby. A minute later, I treaded water beneath the bow. The ship, a nine-meter skimmer, blazed. Something must have gone wrong with its fire deterrent protocols. Another mighty wave smashed the boat. The stern dipped down into the water, but the hungry flames seemed immune to the deluge.

I heard a voice.

My auditory receptors picked up a low moan under the snap crackle of the fire and the steady pounding of the rain and waves. I followed the sound, swimming around the bow to the port side of the boat. A neon-lit life jacket bobbed in the black expanse. I jetted to the object. My system wound tight as I latched on and spun the person to face me.

Hassan. Kuta's friend/other bodyguard/pain in my flesh-covered ass.

His eyes were closed, and his overlarge forehead looked bruised.

"Where's Kuta!" I yelled.

He moaned and mumbled. Damn. Adding the facts together pointed to a possible attack. The Cheng family were ambassadors for the greater government for the North Asian Republic and under constant death and kidnapping threat from groups of insurrectionists, those who didn't like being forced into the republic, those who favored universal rights for all sentient beings, those who hated the *haves*. Basically, ninety percent of the population.

Kuta was especially vulnerable. I'd already saved him from an attack on his life at the Facility F Military School. It appeared his family's enemies had tried again.

And perhaps succeeded.

A deeper fear screwed into my processor and created a physical pain where a human heart would've been. This eclipsed the fear for myself. This was Kuta. My friend. My charge. My... I couldn't put a name to it. Kuta shone like a star in my universe, and if something happened to him... I stopped myself from conjecturing. Only logic and quick action could help him right now.

I searched for any sign of Kuta and pulled Hassan along, his floatation device keeping his head just above water. Any human riding on a watercraft wore a small necklace that instantly expanded upon emersion in water. The lifesaver stayed buoyant indefinitely, glowed neon orange, and emitted a signal for rescue boats.

Droids could be retrieved at any time and didn't have a life to lose. Yet ceasing to function and cyber brain damage seemed pretty bad to me, but my security system designer had not asked my opinion.

Kuta would've worn one. But he may have been injured in the explosion, or the lifesaver could've failed. If he was even on the boat. Uncertainty plagued me. Yet my reasoning was sound. Where Hassan and I were, Kuta was sure to be.

I visually scanned the waters with standard droid vision of 40X40 with magnification. No clue as to Kuta's whereabouts. Was he still aboard, or was this a wild red herring chase? Mixed metaphors. But I didn't have time to search my DL for a better description.

My power level plummeted, and I struggled to hold Hassan against the tempest. Recharging in sunlight didn't present an issue, but in the darkness, it took everything to stay afloat.

The boat slid underwater. The waves finally extinguishing the last of the flames. I hadn't seen any movement. I determined the smoke and flames would have killed anyone who remained long before the boat went under. My emotional chip tightened my chest and my tendons. Damn my feelings. They weren't helping.

Kuta may not have even been on board. But that silly illogical thought impulse shot through my awareness again.

Kuta *had* been aboard, and I had failed to save him.

I floated in the blackness with Hassan in tow. The emotional waves were almost worse than the pounding of the black water. I considered letting go and dropping like a boulder to the bottom of the ocean. Yet I could not. I would not. With or without Kuta. I desired to continue to exist. I had no love for Hassan, but he was a living being, and Kuta would want me to help him.

I considered my next actions. Waiting for rescue appeared at the top of the list.

That plan didn't seem wise. Kuta and the entire Cheng family were under constant threat, and a ship with him on it would be a ripe target. Perhaps their enemies had created the disaster.

Staying at the wreckage location was not advisable.

I picked a direction and started swimming. Because life, organic or not, was too precious to waste.

Somewhere in my old DLs, I found a megabyte of info concerning survival skills. Sifu—my maternal figure, master, and the human on whose brain pattern mine was based—had seen fit to give me detailed information about how to survive being lost at sea. The information scrolled, and I dissected the megabytes through the harsh slap of rain. Thank the makers for Sifu and her over preparation for every contingency.

My last mission had been in a desert at Facility F, deep in the Sahara. When did she think I might be lost at sea? But she did consider everything. A longing gripped my mind. The day and hour remained unknown, but I knew I hadn't seen her in a long time. The details scrambled when I tried to grasp them like any of my recent information.

Potential dangers included the weather, my limited energy, and sea predators. The troubles would expand as our time in the water extended. My energy level shot to the top of my concerns. It had decreased to thirty percent. If my power reached critical, I'd be fish food, and Hassan wouldn't be far behind.

I searched my list of options and decided to follow the current. From my download, currents usually moved in the direction of land. I powered forward, pulling Hassan's head back so the continuous waves wouldn't drown him.

The water temperature increased. I sighed. At least my thermometer gauge still functioned.

I pushed away fear that threatened to squish me like a recycling compactor and focused my attention on just moving my arms and legs in a rhythm. I pulled out my old mantra. *Namaste. Stroke. Namaste. Stroke.*

I saw and heard nothing indicating rescue was on the way. Maybe I should've stayed at the wreckage site. Even Kuta's enemies might have shown mercy and taken us aboard. Now we may be condemned to a watery death.

My heads-up display of time remaining flashed red, and claws of panic tightened my system. I didn't know if the human version of panic was this horrible, but if it was, I wanted it removed.

Time remaining until total system shut down: 23 minutes 20 seconds.

The water warmed to exactly 39 degrees Celsius, a clear indicator that I approached a landmass, but nothing appeared in my visuals.

I ran an analysis: chance of rescue 0.0582 percent in this weather, chance of locating a body of land with my drained energy 0.1006 percent.

In the distance, a bolt of electricity lit the sky in an atrial pattern against the bank of dark clouds in a spectacular display. I'd never witnessed a storm of this magnitude unleashed. If another strike landed close to us, it'd deep-fry my systems.

A creepy-crawly sensation spread in my nervous system. The clouds built up for another blast. Not more than 200 meters away, the lightning touched the water.

Power infused my body. If it had been a small shock, and if I hadn't already been damaged, I might have been able to withstand the jolt. But neither was true.

Shut down imminent.

With my last ounce of awareness, I released Hassan so he would have a chance. My heads-up display darkened, and I slid beneath the waves.

The sun warmed my chassis and recharged my batteries. Powering with solar energy spread a special kind of heat that being charged at a charging station didn't. Warm, comforting, natural. I functioned like a real human who ate sunshine instead of food.

I allowed my systems to come online. My memory warbled back in flashes of data. The boat, the water, Hassan, sinking. I opened my eyes and jumped.

An expanse of beach surrounded me. White sands stretched at least two kilometers in each direction. Any indication that there had been a storm or fire or life-threatening towers of water had vanished, replaced with cloudless, blue skies and gently rolling waves.

But how had I gotten here?

My last memory clip consisted of my vision blanking and the press of the sea on my flesh. I checked my internal systems. I'd suffered a cranial injury, but other than that, my flesh and chassis were operational, which shouldn't be. My skin should've deteriorated without oxygen. So, I couldn't have been under more than thirty minutes.

I searched the beach with my unenhanced sensors. Frustrating. I was accustomed to 4-D, x-ray, magnifying sensors that ranged for kilometers. Human-style visuals were a shade more potent than being blind. I wobbled onto my feet. My renewed power had only reached my most important systems, equilibrium not among my vital systems. I staggered but maintained my footing and visually scanned the beach and shore for any sign that Hassan had survived.

I detected human footprints.

Shoe size 40 European, currently barefoot, weight approximately 70 kg from the depths of the impressions. The steps followed a direct path from my position to the palm-dotted tree line.

Someone had assisted me. Whether for good or ill, I didn't know. Could it be Hassan? The footprints seemed too small, but I could be incorrect. My cyber brain still labored at self-repair. Whoever it was, I would locate them, and together we'd plan next steps.

I looked back out at the distant horizon, searching for indications of life or rescue. Nothing. Water met sky in an infinite line across the horizon. I evaluated my external chassis. I wore my loose, gray fatigue pants and a bikini top. Bruises dotted my flesh but no permanent damage. My external appearance was that of a seventeen-year-old girl, a bit ruffled, but the same as always. Well, except for the deep scar on the left side of my face, but after six months, that was normal too.

I ran my fingers through my hair. The strands were filled with sand and tangled. Gross. I shook it out and wrapped it in a loose bun on top of my head using a clasp I found in my pocket. The downside of having a human exterior. Maintenance.

I traced the path of footprints. I'd only taken a half dozen steps when my audio picked up stirring in the underbrush.

Was the island inhabited? Could it be a wild animal? Or perhaps a droid doing border control? The fact I had no information sent a wave of cool fear through my emotional chip. I braced myself, even though I couldn't have fought off a pride of kittens and attempted my tough look.

It wasn't Hassan, or an animal, or even a droid.

He was instantly recognizable, same disheveled dark hair and intelligent black eyes, standing before me with arms filled with unripe coconuts.

Kuta.

I used what little power I had to close the distance between us. He'd been dead.

I'd been sure he was dead, but he was still alive. I didn't care that we hadn't had close physical contact since our time in Facility F. My emotional chip overruled my logic center. I flung myself at him, wrapping my arms around his neck. The coconuts flew from his arms.

He grabbed me into a tight embrace and lifted me off my feet. His body warm and taut against mine, I closed my eyes and let the intense feedback course through my system. Happiness, relief, surprise, and something else. I didn't want to explore the last feeling too deeply. I'd always found Kuta visually and emotionally pleasing since the first moment I saw him on the train traveling to the Egypt territory. But he had not shown any sensual interest in me after finding out my droid status.

This moment felt different.

His body heat rose, and his grip on my flesh tightened as he exhaled in my ear.

"Zee! I'm so glad you're okay."

The palm trees, the beach, the waves faded from my attention, and a flutter coursed over my skin from my head to the tips of my toes. I leaned back to look in his eyes. "I thought you were dead."

A slight smile slid across his face, but he didn't speak. He also didn't release me. The warmth and tension increased, and the urge to lean in and kiss him thundered in my mind. I resisted. He had to make the move. I was his bodyguard and a non-bonded android. I could be reading the signals wrong. My protocols declared that he had to initiate sensual contact.

He waited for 2.1 seconds more and put me down on my feet. I remained in his loose embrace for another second until he released me and sighed.

"I saw you this morning when the storm broke," Kuta said. "Well, I saw something caught on the outer corals. The waves must have washed you here.

You looked—I don't know the right word. Broken? I hoped you would recover, and you did."

The term broken sent a negative feedback loop through me. Perhaps he did think of me as just a droid. A broken thing. I allowed the feeling to dissipate—at least he'd been glad to see me.

"What happened? How did you get here?" he asked.

"I ran out of energy fighting the storm and the waves with…" The recollection of Hassan tumbled back. "I tried to save Hassan, but I cut him loose because I was afraid I'd drag him under. I'm sorry."

I'd failed. First to save Kuta then to assist Hassan. I proved as bad a bodyguard droid as I'd been a spy droid.

Kuta's face screwed up, and he grabbed my elbow in a tight grip.

"Don't be sorry. If anyone should be sorry, it should be—" He released me, stepped back, and tilted his head. "We can search the island for him. He may have washed in as well."

We scoured the beach for any sign of Hassan. Hours later, my renewed power dipped to unsafe levels, and Kuta showed signs of exhaustion. He'd been silent during our search, eyes squinting, taking in every detail of the coastline.

Rocks and sandbars jutted into the ocean from the path ahead like giant fingers. The island sprawled larger than I'd anticipated, but any kind of distance scanning was still impossible.

Kuta climbed the uneven terrain, turning to give me a hand.

Usually, I wouldn't have needed the assistance, but with my low energy level and my internal repair nanobots sucking up backup power, my balance was dicey at best. I smiled at him, and he squeezed my hand. A warm blast of electrons hummed in my system. Being with Kuta, stranded and in danger or not, was wonderful.

We reached another stretch of beach. At last, I decided to broach a question.

"How did you get here? Did the storm wash you this way, too?"

His eyes shifted, and he looked at the sand beneath us. "I grabbed a lifeboat, and it took me to the nearest landmass. I tried to find you both, but there was no sign of you. Then the explosion happened, and everything got confused."

Kuta's body language was strange, but I made the logical assumption that he felt guilty for making it to the lifeboat while Hassan and I didn't. My memory still blank from that period, I had no confirmation of what had occurred on the boat.

He stumbled but hid it well. Exhaustion pulled on him as low power pulled on me. We needed to redirect our energies.

"We've looked at every logical place for Hassan, and we can search again later. What matters is staying alive. Have you done any recon to the island's interior to determine if there are inhabitants? We should establish a safe perimeter. Then we'll need to find shelter and a water source." I wanted to take it back immediately. Since my emotional chip still spiraled in turmoil from the close physical contact, I'd reverted to military speak.

He just laughed and gave me one of his circuit-frying smiles. "I don't know about recon or perimeters, but I walked into the tree line and searched for some water and food. I haven't seen anyone. It's so peaceful." He didn't sound panicked or perturbed by our castaway status.

"Peaceful can still be dangerous. I was damaged during the sinking and—"

"I'm sorry." It was unusual for him to be apologetic for something he had no fault in. He was usually full of confidence and positivity. But traumatic experiences inspired strange reactions in humans.

It was time for action, not condolences, and it was up to me to provide motivation. I was still very low on power, and Kuta, as a completely organic being, had basic survival to consider. "Safety. Fresh water. Food. Shelter," I spouted the order without thinking too much.

"Yes, Captain Zee!" He saluted me.

I laughed. "Sorry, I just want to make sure you're taken care of. It's my job, you know."

His expression sobered. "I found some coconuts and fruit. And there are a ton of resources on the rescue raft. I'll show you."

He led the way down the beach to a sheltered alcove. A thin sheen of sweat formed on his golden skin accentuating his taut muscles. My sensual stirrings from earlier awakened. I had the architecture of a droid but the mind-mapping of a human and a good deal of emotional-based physical reactions.

My original chassis was that of a companion droid after all. Not that I'd ever delved into that facet of myself.

Well, I'd had that moment with Kuta in the water tower. I would've definitely liked to explore more, but I wasn't sure what he thought of it or me. I knew he appreciated me saving him from Facility F. Hell, he'd given me a job and saved my mom, but beyond that lay a dangerous, unexplored territory full of emotional landmines.

Kuta halted, and his mouth hung open. "No," he whispered. His head whipped back and forth.

"What's wrong?" I feared I knew the answer.

"The raft... The raft is gone," his voice took on a heartbroken tone that made me want to gather him into my arms, but I maintained my decorum.

"Are you sure we're in the right spot?"

"Positive." He walked up closer to a sharp outcropping and smoothed a finger over the stone. "High tide must have taken it. I know I tied it here."

I did a visual recon of the beach and detected no sign of footprints, but my current abilities were only slightly better than a human's perception. Most of my advanced functions were still offline. Damn it.

Together, we examined the location, eyes locked on the water line, searching for clues about the raft. It would've been neon orange and easy to spot at a distance. Kuta was overheating, and I was unsteady. I still needed more recouping time before I put more physical stress on my body. But his body was my responsibility, so I pushed on.

"Can you access the Cortex?" Kuta fidgeted, uncomfortable asking me about my special skills.

"If I were at maximum capacity then maybe, but this is a largely unpopulated area without a lot of access coverage. And my memory is compromised. I believe it was during the storm. In the last vidclip I have, we were at your home in the Northern Province. I don't recall even boarding a boat."

He seemed genuinely shocked. His eyes widened, and he grabbed my hand again and squeezed. "Will you... uh... get better?" He stuttered, searching for the proper phrase, and I laughed.

"I might be able to re-download the memories, or once my internal repair is complete, I may retrieve them myself from backup storage. You can tell me all I missed while we search for a clean water source."

He nodded, absorbing my status update without obvious repulsion. He'd been accepting of me since finding out I was a droid. I wondered how far that acceptance reached. Did he think of me as just a machine or as a girl? I knew how I felt about him. The sun reflecting on him made him look like a shiny, Greek statue that I had a strange desire to lick.

I didn't comprehend the urge fully, but it sent a spray of electrons over my skin.

I shook my head to clear out the invading images and pulled him toward the more wooded area of the island. I'd learned from my survival download, if we find a body of moving water, it could be drinkable, and fresh water would be away from the beach area.

"How far back do you remember?" he asked.

"I remember patrolling the perimeter at your home in the North Province. The last day that's clear was..." I had to stop walking and slow my spotty vid clip files to make any sense of the images. "You and your mom were arguing about a new school in the New Zealand province." *Again*, I added silently. They seemed like a close family, but they had very different opinions.

"Yeah, you're not missing much then. Maybe a few days?"

"That's a relief."

"So, she insisted I go to another high security, tight-assed, secondary school to learn all the *important* things while I'm protected. She didn't like it when I brought up I'd nearly been killed at my last school. She said I had to go. I said no. She sent me anyway. A normal Tuesday night." He sounded flippant, amused, but even my impaired abilities picked up on the undercurrent of pain and anger suffusing his tone.

"Oh, Kuta. I'm sorry. At least she let you bring me. And Hassan."

I allowed the feeling of guilt to surface for a nanosecond then crammed it down. I'd tried everything to help Hassan and almost found a watery grave myself, but still, I wished I'd been able to save him.

Kuta nodded and averted his eyes. We walked for a few minutes, birdcalls and buzzing filling the air.

A black cloud of undulating insects approached us. I identified them as mosquitos. They swarmed every exposed bit of skin on Kuta and me. I had a small amount of blood that kept my flesh healthy, and the insects didn't seem to mind that it came from an android. Kuta batted furiously at his arms and legs.

"Damn, there's no end to them. Come on!" He moved as fast as the dense underbrush would allow, me trailing, letting him set the pace. The insects remained a nuisance, and new batches joined.

I scrolled through options of how to escape or avoid becoming a bug pincushion. An old DL gave me what I needed. I used my internal audio to set off a high-pitched humming that would deter the tiny winged monsters. They were mere annoyances to me but carried multiple human-infecting diseases. I closed my eyes and redirected energy to set a perimeter around us, creating a bug-free zone.

"Hey, they're going away," he said.

I opened my eyes.

He stared at me. "You're doing something."

"Just call me the bug zapper," I said, trying to add some levity.

"Is there anything you can't do?" Kuta chuckled.

"Sew," I said. Although I probably could if DLed the proper information.

He laughed again. It was good to see his smile in the midst of this emergency. The old Kuta back at last.

The energy output for using my abilities absorbed much of my reserve, and I swayed again. Kuta leaped to my side to steady me.

"You okay?" His concerned voice sent an arrow of emotion through me. I'd have to examine it later, but it reminded me of happiness.

"I'll be fine. My reserves are very low, and it's difficult to maintain a wide bug barrier."

He placed an arm around me and supported my weight with the other. "There. Now I can help you, and you can help me." He flashed his perfect smile, and we set off.

The feeling of having his slightly warmed, golden skin against mine triggered my intimacy protocols. I had to thrust away the desire to throw him to the jungle floor and touch every inch of him.

My primary purpose was companionship, hardwired into my chassis, and Kuta's pheromone level must have been extremely elevated to affect me so profoundly. Without my advanced sensors, the exact amount remained unknown, but even my basic abilities of detection urged me to respond. My

emotional chip heartily agreed. But again, logic reared her ugly head. He hadn't said he wanted anything but protection and possibly friendship.

And with my programming, I had to wait for him to make a romantic move.

If he ever did.

That thought process made me sad, so I refocused on the purpose of our jungle excursion. Water.

Mosquitoes were a sign of nearby water. I hoped the source was more than the small stagnant dips in the ground we'd seen so far.

"What's that sound?" Kuta asked, voice filled with controlled excitement.

I'd been so distracted, I hadn't noticed the low rumble. Running water. We hobbled faster. To his credit, his body language said he wanted to hurry and find what was making the sound, but he carefully assisted me through the brush until we broke into a clearing.

A secluded grotto sprawled before us with a waterfall cascading down a rough cliff. The pool seemed to have been carved out of the rock itself. Melati putih, commonly known as jasmine, perfumed the air, and magenta and violet moon orchids decorated the edges of the water.

The area was breathtaking. If I had breath to take.

Kuta sucked in air, held it for a beat, and breathed out. "Amazing. Now if the water is—"

"Clean," I finished. "Help me down to the edge, and I'll test it. E coli can't hurt me." I smiled at him, and he grinned back, shaking his head.

"You are very handy to have around when stranded on a deserted island. Did you know that?"

"Yep." I had no qualms about my skills. I was a badass. I knew for human conversation I should tone down my bravado, but I played it for humor, and it worked. I got another laugh.

"Not lacking in self-confidence. Are you?"

"Nope." I continued the joke, but inside my insecurities raged. Mostly about my facial injury. Kuta had offered to repair my broken skin since I had received the injury saving his life, but I'd refused. He had done so much already. Hiring me. Transporting Sifu into hiding from the NAR government, which still wanted both of us dead or in custody. Making the target on the Cheng family even bigger than before the attempt on Kuta's life.

I couldn't ask for more. My current function didn't require a completely human facade. My only regret was the constant reminder that I was *other* than Kuta.

And really no one was like me.

Together, we negotiated the steep incline to the water's edge. It was rocky with large, jagged stones barring the path, but soon we stood ready for the test.

I crouched down. The water was pristine and blue. In this area, the trees had not grown in the rocky soil, so the sun bounced against the water in sections, turning it golden. It reflected in Kuta's eyes as he watched me take a mouthful.

It tasted like water from a well, full of many discernible compounds such as calcium, but no dangerous bacteria, or such a small amount as to not be detected by my internal sensor.

"It's good to drink," I said.

He whooped and cannonballed into the deep end. A thousand internal warnings bells sounded.

He erupted from the water and slicked his hair back out of his eyes.

"There could be venomous animals!" I yelled. "There could be rocks! There could be—"

"Or there could be nothing to worry about. You should join me." His tone deepened, and I felt myself wanting nothing more than to jump right in next to him. Swimming with Kuta was fun. I'd done it before. The memory sent a flush to my face.

"Someone should stay on land and guard." My voice dipped and said but-I-really-want-to-jump-in.

"We've searched the island, Zee. We're alone. And I'm in danger in here all by myself. The bugs will suck me dry."

I snorted slightly. Charming as usual.

And the bugs *were* targeting him. I dove into the pool. Even without my full capacity, my visual assessment told me the lagoon was deep enough for me not to worry about hitting bottom. The water cooled my skin since I hadn't been able to use my internal regulator. Wonderful. And the sun blazing down supplied me with energy without overheating my workings. In short, it felt pretty damn awesome.

Kuta swam over to tread water near me. "Do you do everything well? That was an amazing dive."

"I think we've established I have many skills." I loved it when he noticed me. Which in the last few months he often did, but that was all. Noticed, not touched.

"Safety and water. Check, check. Only things left are food and shelter."

"Both those should be attainable when I reach full charge. Don't worry."

"I'm never worried when I'm with you. You're like a superhero, Zee."

My rhythmic breathing hitched, and I had to nudge my processor to continue the protocol. What he was saying registered as extremely positive. I could take it as a go signal if only he would make his move. I sighed. It must be my face.

"A superhero that should be wearing a mask," I said, trying to joke about my situation. Humans did it often to obscure things that caused them pain. Some said it helped with the emotion. It really, really didn't. But I maintained a light tone.

"Zeeeeee," Kuta said. "You're beautiful. The most beautiful girl… android… I've ever seen. With or without your scar." He reached out to where the human skin had peeled back and stroked my chin beneath it. Laser thrills of sensation jolted me as if I'd touched a live wire.

"Does it hurt?" he asked.

"No." Was all I could muster. My voice constricted as if I really needed air and I couldn't quite get it.

He leaned closer. This was it. From the thousands of romantic vidclips I'd DLed, I could feel it. He was going to kiss me, and boy, oh boy, did I want him to.

Instead, Kuta grabbed my shoulders and pulled me through the water toward the shore. He pushed me out and followed quickly.

"Wh-what's wrong. Did I do something wrong?" The place where my heart should've been experienced a slash of pain. Oh, those programmers really did do their job too well.

"No! No. Look." He turned me and pointed up to the peak behind us. At the apex, small stones were crumbling, and above it, a larger rock wobbled in the light breeze. If it had fallen, it could've caused grievous injury to both of us. If my sensors had been working, I would've detected it and not allowed Kuta to be in danger. I'd almost gotten him killed.

"I'm so sorry. With my current level of damage, I didn't…"

"Zee! I just noticed it. I'm allowed to save you, too. Right?" He winked, and some of the weight pressing on me subsided. But if I had stayed on shore. If I'd have done visual recon, he wouldn't have to be vigilant.

That was literally my job.

Until I was sure of all the variables on the island, I had to stay on task and not allow Kuta to distract me. "It's my duty to protect you. I won't lapse again."

The emotion cooled. He rolled his lips in and bit them closed, exhaled, and remained silent.

"Did you get enough hydration?" I asked.

"Yeah." His arms were crossed, and he looked away from me.

How had our connection crumbled so quickly? I shook off the emotion which clung to me, sadness mostly, and got to business. Kuta liked action, and I was going to keep him too busy to be upset with me.

"On to food. When was the last time you ate?"

"On board the ship. You were there at dinner."

"Sorry, memory issues." I hated having the blank. Could something I'd forgotten point to what happened on the boat? Boats sank so rarely with the current designs that it lit my suspicions. And how had I ended up in the water before the explosion? These were the questions I needed answered.

"Forgot." He chuckled.

I joined him, and the tension broke.

"I found some coconuts back on the beach," he said. "I know they're edible."

I recalled the color and size.

"Not ripe yet. There'd be very little meat and some thin water. Come on. I have a better idea." A Cortex connection proved impossible, so the exact hour was a mystery, but from the position of the sun, it was still just mid-morning. We had time to find shelter and create a fire.

We reached the beach and found a sandbar. "You stay here. Numerous dangerous predators lurk around the shore sharks and jellyfish. I will return with food."

"I'm going to find some kindling for a fire." He entered the tree line and set to looking for dry wood.

I waded into the calm water and surveyed for fish. How quickly the sea had transformed. Tsunami driven whitecaps to gentle waves, life to death, all could change in a microsecond. My injury had reinforced to me that existence wasn't a given and could be removed at any moment.

Standing still, I waited, shoulders tense, searching.

"How long until dinner?" Kuta yelled from the trees with an armload of kindling.

I groaned, and my shoulders dipped. "Forever unless you learn to be quiet. Now hush."

He hushed.

Fish and other marine creatures returned and slowly surrounded me. I couldn't categorize them all without a Cortex connection, but some were in my general DL memory. The majority I judged too small, but then I saw the yellow, striped creature. I targeted him.

Triggerfish. Edible. Over 150 grams. Perfect.

I waited until the exact moment he drifted to within five centimeters, and I snapped my arm downward and made a grab.

I missed.

How had I missed? I was fast enough. I had calculated the probability of his direction and narrowed it down to the most likely path.

"No food?" Kuta asked using a wistfully, sad voice.

"Shut up, Kuta. I got this."

Without any outside research, I had to dig back into my DLs and seek out any references to fish and fishing. I scrolled through thousands of techniques and deduced that the water density had thrown off my calculations. My processor moved like molasses and would until my battery fully recharged. But I would have time for that later. Kuta needed to eat.

I allowed twenty-seven seconds to slide by. The fish returned mostly small non-edible varieties. I spied new prey. My processor took .5 seconds to get the calculation exactly right. I snatched the fish from the water, and it wiggled out of my fingers.

Spinning, I eyed Kuta, but he just gave me a thumbs-up. At least he wasn't mocking me. I hadn't considered the slick exterior. I sighed. I had a great capacity for both companionship and war, but none, it would seem, for fishing.

Fourteen seconds ticked by. I allowed the biggest fish yet to brush against the flesh of my lower leg before I lunged and snatched the creature hard enough to hold him.

I may not be a natural at fishing, but I was a fast learner. I smiled and thrust the fish into the air.

Kuta pumped his fist. "Well done!"

My face flushed with a wash of heat. I enjoyed Kuta's attention and adulation. I brought the fish back to the shore and placed it on a stone.

"What is it?" Kuta wrinkled his nose.

"Edible and, from what my records indicate, delicious once cooked."

Kuta laughed. "Works for me. I got this dry tinder from the beach and the woods." He gave me his proud smile.

"Looks like we make a good team."

"If only we had an ignitor. I had something on the boat, but... I'm sure there's a way to light them. Rubbing sticks together or something. I can't quite remember from my Explorer Camp days."

"Explorer Camp?"

"Yeah, even when I was small, my parents were always shipping me off as far from them as they could."

Bitterness flowed under his light demeanor, and I let the line of questioning drop. "I'm going to try something. It might not work. My power is very low."

"I'll take your try over other people's sure thing."

Ever the charmer. I repaid his compliment with a closed-mouth grin and made a small triangle with the dry kindling. I had heaters in my fingers, which reached temperatures in excess of 150 degrees Celsius. I focused on my hands, and the heat pooled in my digits. My fingers hovered over the twigs, and I let a burst of energy escape my reserves. The sticks flamed and caught quickly. But my head grew fuzzy like I'd gotten too big a DL all at once, swimmy and unfocused. I'd been crouching and suddenly lost my balance. I tipped backward.

Kuta dove and caught me. He slid beneath me and lowered me to the ground. Another jolt of his closeness scrambled my processor. He smelled of musky boy, and all I wanted was for him to lean down and put those soft lips against mine.

He met my eyes, and we held the look for a long moment. His heart rate jacked to over 125 bpm. He was definitely experiencing similar emotions, or at least his body was attracted to me.

What about his mind? What was he thinking? What about the future? My logic circuit whispered. I told it to shut the hell up.

But he had to break the physical barrier. He was close. I sensed him leaning in. He closed his eyes. My nervous system sent a pleasant thrill through my circuits. My backup energy flashed. I was too late.

Emergency shutdown blinked in big red letters over my internal display. My head fell back, and my vision went dark.

❖

My external senses returned. I was laying on something soft, and my batteries had rebounded, but the solar energy had dimmed.

Damn. Damn. Damn. Damn. Infinity damn. Why did my energy bottom out right when Kuta was about to give in to his attraction? All I wanted was to feel like a normal girl. Or at least as close as I could come. To feel *good*. And my dumb system had betrayed me.

I cracked one eye open. The sun hung low over the water, sending strips of orange, red, and lavender over the rolling surface. Next to me, a fire crackled. Kuta had taken advantage of the spark I'd set and fed the flames. He sat on the opposite side of the fire. He didn't notice that I was awake yet, so I had a chance to observe him.

One knee up, he rested his elbow on it and cradled his chin with his hand. His perma-smile had melted into a quiet, serious face that was just as, or more, attractive than his grin. I felt that the smile was often for show, and this was what lay underneath. A young, heartbreakingly beautiful man who had serious thoughts in his head.

He stared into the flame as if the fire might have the answer to some of his questions. Maybe it did for humans. I saw beautiful lights and varying degrees of heat. My sensors must have been somewhat repaired, as I detected the heat of the fire at exactly 100 degrees Celsius. But no mystical answers.

I rose to a sitting position, and Kuta stirred, his smile returning. His eyes crinkled.

"Hey there. How are you feeling?" Kuta asked.

"Like I wrestled a crocodile."

His face lit up and quickly fell. "And how would you know how that feels? You haven't actually—"

"No, but I searched my DL's and discovered accounts and found a good analogy."

He laughed again. "You are endlessly fascinating, Zee."

The island had grown chilly in the dusk, yet Kuta still didn't have a shirt on. He had bundled it up under my head to give me a pillow. He had taken care of me when I collapsed. My emotions whirled and twisted.

"Are you going to be okay?" he asked. "Is there anything I can do?"

"I have regained an eighteen percent charge, but with the sun down, it won't last long. My internal repair nanobots are sapping a lot of my energy right now. In a few days, if the sun continues to shine, I should be 100 percent."

"Look, we really need to talk. I don't know how long we're going to be stuck here. You can't be overtaxing yourself. I know you're a droid, and you're my… employee. Or my parents' employee. Anyway, you're also my friend, and I expect you to take care of yourself. We can get through this. Together."

His concern touched me, and I had to examine the tone and double meaning and pauses. Nuances of human interaction still gave me virtual hives. But I got a general warm glow from what he was saying.

A myriad of words cued up in my processor to say, but I went with the safe and sincere, "Thank you, Kuta."

He nodded, and the conversation dropped for a moment. We could be stuck on the island for a while, and that increased the danger to both of us. Was anyone even looking for us?

"When were we supposed to arrive?" I asked. "I can't even connect to the Cortex to determine month, day, or time."

He shifted to lay lengthwise in front of the fire, like a lithe, jungle animal.

I took a vidcap for future reference.

"Do you think Mom has given up yet?" He sounded almost hopeful.

"No, of course not. You're her child. My Sifu would do anything to find me. And I'd do anything for her." I had been repressing my deep sadness about the lack of her in my life. It was for the best for her to be in hiding. Yet I still thought of her every day.

Kuta snorted. "I haven't seen any sign of a rescue by air, sea, or carrier pigeon. And I don't know if I mind."

A list of probable reasons why we hadn't seen anything scrolled through my cyber brain. The primary being, there were thousands of islands in the Indonesian archipelago. And it could take weeks for the volatile countries of the area to allow a rescue attempt. Even NAR itself had open rebellions and Droid Rights Riots raging on the mainland. Resources for the outer reaches were scarce. Even for a diplomat's missing son.

I knew he didn't want to hear that. Logic didn't matter when emotions hit.

"But should we start a signaling effort?" I asked. "I've had no luck contacting the Cortex. The locater in your lifejacket doesn't work. Maybe the one in your rescue boat is working even if it floated offshore. It could be—"

"It wasn't."

That answer came surprisingly fast, and my eyebrows quirked.

His eyes flicked to the water. "I checked it before it drifted away."

His vitals elevated—heart rate increasing, eyes blinking. He must feel very guilty about losing it. And I still feared even mentioning Hassan's name for fear of triggering Kuta's grief response. I'd search the coast again as soon as possible.

"We shouldn't put out a call, anyway. I'd prefer to lie low," he said. "It's too big a risk to send a general distress message. Especially for you."

"True. I'm technically AWOL," I said.

He shook his head and stood, clenching his hands into fists. "As if you had joined their kill-squads yourself." He growled low in the back of his throat. "They created you to work for them without giving you an option, then would punish you for leaving. I'm tempted to join the resistance."

I crisscrossed my legs and looked up at him. He really was dreamy when he was being heroic. "They're losing from all reports. Badly." Old news vidcap played in my mind, and I cringed. "Stripping flesh from droids and wiping their brains. And the humans that take up the cause… Well, it's good we're here and away from the fighting."

The war on the mainland seemed like a DL about the early twenty-first century. The vidcaps of all the carnage, blood, body parts, and gore, while horrible, seemed almost unreal. I was glad to be far from the war zone. Yet those images replayed and stirred my system, tightened my joints, sent a flash of negative feedback. A part of me itched to do something. But what? What could one droid do in the big scheme of things? I wasn't even sure where I fit in. I felt like a human. Eighty-eight percent of the time I thought like a human. Yet I knew how the world saw me, especially with my facial injury. Pure droid. Non-organic life. Worthless.

And if NAR ever caught me, I'd *want* to stop functioning. Everyone knew what they did to traitors.

At least Kuta treated me like I mattered.

"I'd love to fight," he said. "But I can't. As if I could do anything but what my family wants." His body temp rose, and his muscles tightened. He'd always resented the limitations of his family's position, but this seemed more pronounced than usual.

"Once you're of age, you'll have many options. Don't discount the power of your position," I said. People liked Kuta and respected his family and their financial and political power.

"All I want…" He paused and cleared his throat. "We're doing well so far. Taking a chance on opening an emergency signal doesn't seem wise." No smile. No eye contact. He appeared upset at me, and I wasn't sure why.

He nestled next to me, our hips touching and put an arm around me. "Is this okay?"

My skyrocketing emotional chip blasted happy, positive ions through my system. Okay? Hell. Yes. I didn't trust my voice not to betray my excitement at being so close. So intimate. And he had initiated it! I nodded and leaned in.

Sitting quietly by the fire in his arms defined the term bliss to me. If a droid could experience bliss.

In the morning, a few hours after first light, my battery was half charged, which wasn't bad considering I had a massive internal self-repair ongoing.

Limited scanning returned; I breathed a sigh of relief. Being without my extended sensors was akin to being blind. I reached out to the Cortex but still couldn't pick up a link. Damn. If I could access my cloud backup, my memories of the last week should return. But that wouldn't happen until I picked up a strong signal, maybe not until we reached civilization.

If we reached civilization.

I subverted the worry that wanted to take a foothold in my system. Being on the island had been tolerable so far. More than that. I reviewed my moments with Kuta. It had been more like a fantasy than a tragedy.

Eventually, I'd have to determine the best escape route that didn't alert hostile forces to our whereabouts. But that wasn't right now. Right now, the general area was clear of danger, the sunrise made the water look like molten gold, and Kuta was sleeping peacefully at my side.

His lips were full and looked soft. I ran a simulation of kissing him. Strange emotions stirred within me. I knew he was a human, and I was just a droid, and his employee at that, but pretending wasn't forbidden.

He opened his eyes and caught me staring. I quickly averted my eyes, loosened my hair from its bun, and started to braid.

"Good morning, Zee. Do you need help with that?"

"Huh?" I definitely sounded like a super-intelligent, multimillion credit droid. Not.

"I do it for my sister. Here. Let me." He sat up and pulled my hair to the back and, working with quick and decisive motions, he plaited my hair.

I had never realized the act of touching someone's hair could be sensual. Sure, I had DLs of human reactions to scalp stimuli, but I didn't think I could have a reaction. I was wrong. His hand brushed the skin on my half-bare back, and my breathing hitched.

"Your hair is so beautiful and fine. Silky even."

"It's partially made from silk." I shouldn't have said it. He was thinking of me as a human, and that was what I wanted. Now I had him thinking of me as a machine again. Stupid. Stupid droid.

"They did a wonderful job." He laid a warm hand on my shoulder. "Do you have anything to secure it?"

I handed to a clasp to him. He finished the job and turned me to face him. "Beautiful. As always."

I smiled, and my protocols flushed my cheeks.

"You're also cute when you blush." He stood up and brushed sand from his shorts. "I'll be back in a moment."

"Where are you going? I should go with you."

"No. Not this time. Some things a man has to do alone."

I wasn't good at subtext, but I finally understood. He had to eliminate.

Naturally. Why hadn't I sought a logical answer before speaking? I maintained a calm exterior but wanted to shove my face into the sand.

"Be careful of animals. My long-range scanners aren't back online yet, so I can't vet the area properly," I said.

"I'll be careful."

He walked into the underbrush until neither my visual nor my renewed sensors could track him. After a few minutes, I got antsy. So much potential danger. A rabid carnivore, a nest of bugs, a sinkhole. One of the worst things about having a cyber brain was the horrible options that kept scrolling. I stood and took two steps in his direction.

I sensed movement from the brush. Crap. It was Kuta, and he would think I was following him. I scrambled back to the fire, threw myself down, leaned back on my straight arms with my face turned up as if trying to tan my skin. Actual tanning would've been a fruitless endeavor. My pigment would remain the same regardless of its exposure to radiation.

I maintained my nonchalant, solar-charging pose for a few moments, reaching out with my sensors. I should've gotten a good read on Kuta's vitals. Heart rate, blood pressure, temperature.

I detected lizards and a thousand scurrying insects, birds flapping in trees. The sound of shifting foliage continued. My audio told me something big was moving through the brush, but my sensors couldn't get a bead. It was as if there was a large void in the forest.

Sifu, for being a very scientific-minded person, had been superstitious. She read tarot, believed in luck, and in spirits. Which meant because my brain mimicked hers, a part of me also took the supernatural into account. Was it a spirit? Or was my scanner still wonky from the lack of energy and the blow to my head?

My logic circuit wrestled down the fear streaming from my emotional chip. All my consideration had taken .275 seconds but felt at least a hundred times that number. I feared turning. Feared my eyes would show me something I couldn't explain with logic.

I finally swiveled, peered into the dense foliage, and tried to track the source of the anomaly. Squawking

birds fluttered from branch to branch, and teeming insects blanketed the jungle floor. Fronds of palms blew gently in the light breeze off the ocean. No visible danger. No scannable threat. But the tiny hairs on the nape of my neck stood on end.

I targeted the anomaly and entered the vegetation line. I stalked forward, so intent on my goal that I didn't register Kuta until we nearly collided.

"Hey!" He stepped back. "Where's the fire?" He didn't sound annoyed, but I knew it must be strange to find me scrambling after him in the brush.

Strange, weird droid.

A tingling sensation ran over my skin, which was a complete non-standard reaction. It emanated from something other than my logic or even my emotional chip. Foreboding settled over me like a thick blanket of doom, and I did a visual sweep. I reached out further, but the blank area had disappeared.

"Are you okay?" His face did a concerned twist that made my happy impulses dance.

"I thought I detected a presence here, but it wasn't clear, so I was checking it out. But my scanner has been giving me problems."

"Maybe you need more time to repair. Humans and droids alike need time to heal, and I'm the only person out here. Swear. I would've noticed someone else." He winked at me, and my embarrassment grew.

"Sorry. I wanted to make sure you were okay. It's my job."

"You apologize too much. Let's make a pact. We're both here and trying to survive. Let's forget the whole damn human-droid, employee-employer thing. Now we're just two survivors on an island. Helping each other."

I liked the idea, but I didn't like the fact I couldn't count on my own senses. My Sifu-gifted instincts told me something was amiss here, but I couldn't determine what yet. I certainly wasn't going to tell Kuta there was a ghost on the island. I nodded and let myself smile at him.

"We should look for Hassan," Kuta shoulders slumped forward slightly.

I didn't say anything, but another feeling rolled over me. One of hopelessness. We stayed together and walked the entire coastline. No Hassan and no boat. I heard Kuta give an exaggerated sigh three different times. This hunt felt like wasted time, but we had to be sure. Both of us had reasons to feel responsible, but Kuta would be in definite emotional pain. They had been friends for most of their lives.

Kuta stopped when we reached our stretch of beach again. "Nowhere else to look."

"I know. I'm so sorry. He could still be—"

He put up a hand up. "Just give me some time."

"Listen, I'm going to gather some fruit for later."

He kept his eyes on the horizon, so I retreated and did a systematic search for ripe fruit. I cut glances to Kuta, who sank to the sand and placed his forehead on his knees, taking deep breaths. Human grief was an emotion I hoped the programmers had forgotten to include, but I had a sense they hadn't, from the sadness I experienced from missing my Sifu.

I'd accumulated a nice pile of fruit by the time Kuta stood and brushed off his pants. He approached me and took my hand. "I'm thirsty, and it's starting to get hot. Let's go to the watering hole, and we can discuss phase three. Shelter."

"Do you want to talk?" Talking sometimes helped with the grieving process, my DLs assured me.

"No. I just want to do normal stuff and not think about it anymore."

Leading the way, Kuta cut a path to the waterfall. I dashed behind him. I always felt like nothing truly bad could happen when he was near. His presence took the skittery fingers of worry away and made me forget about Hassan, the phantom presence, my faulty sensors, my injured face, and anything but following him.

❖

The next few hours seemed to move faster than my internal timer. Einstein was correct—time was relative. We didn't talk about specifics of our survival or what the plan was or anything important.

He drank water and lay on a large stone, which served as a platform near the edge of the pool.

I lay next to him, absorbing the glorious sun, mere centimeters between us. Being so close and sensing the soft rise and fall of his chest sent a zing of impulses through me. It was exciting but also comfortable to just lay in silence and look at the clear blue sky and let the spray from the waterfall cool our skin. My bikini-top didn't hide much of my skin, which still showed some bruising, but it was healing as my internal injury repaired.

"This is nice." Kuta turned his head to face me.

"Yes, it is." I turned my face too. The tension between us tightened every joint in my body, and my breath grew shallow. Something in my processor mimicked human excitement. My flesh heated, and I waited again for Kuta.

Please. Please. Please.

Again all logic completely shut down when I got this close in proximity to hot, musky-smelling, golden-skinned Kuta.

His breathing was rough, his skin was hot, and I saw his eyes flicker down to my lips. He definitely wanted to kiss me. Probably.

"Do you like me?" Kuta asked.

I laughed so loud that he jumped a little, and I wanted to kick myself down to the beach and race to the lowest depths of the sea. With a sigh, I kept my eyes locked and took the leap. "Of course I like you."

He laughed softly and used a finger to chuck up my chin. Our eyes met, and something like lightning sizzled inside of me.

"Do you want to kiss me?"

Oh. Hell. Yes.

But I couldn't vocalize the words. It was what I'd wanted for six months. I'd thought I'd lost the chance forever. I nodded but gestured to my face. I was damaged. I was a droid.

Did any of that matter to him?

"You're the prettiest, bravest, girl I know. Human or droid. Come here." He grabbed me in a strong grip, and our lips met with tender intensity.

The sensations coursing through my system were similar to the last time we'd kissed. My cyber brain blanked except for his soft lips and hard torso.

Did humans feel with this power? A virtual fire ran over my skin, not to the point of pain but tantalizing and energizing. I clasped his shoulders as if I were drowning. And in a way I was. Wave after wave of sensation crashed over me, pulling me into a vortex I didn't want to escape.

He pulled back for air, and I found myself panting as well. My intimate protocol activated, and all sorts of surprising details trickled into me. Instincts coming online for the first time.

"That was intense." Kuta's eyebrows arched, a smile stretching across his face wider than I'd ever seen.

"Like the first time, only better." I realized that might sound like an insult. I instantly corrected. "Not that the first time was bad. It was amazing." I exhaled harshly. My emotion-overloaded brain wouldn't allow me to find the correct response.

"It's because we really know and like each other now. You know that, right? I really like you, Zee."

I wanted to say *yes*. But until this exact moment, I had been unsure. Hearing him say it aloud felt like the opening of a door to a whole new world.

A world in which I wasn't sure I belonged.

I nodded. I didn't trust my logic circuit or my emotional chip to find the right words. All I wanted was more of Kuta.

My intimate protocol pushed me, made suggestions I longed to attempt. Now that Kuta had broken the touch barrier and expressed his interest, I had more options. I put a finger to his lips to stop him talking and scooted a bit closer, so our bodies touched, but only with the barest brush. I traced his thick lips with the tip of my finger. I knew precisely how many nerve endings I stimulated, and from the sharp intake of breath, so did Kuta.

I leaned in until I was breathing the air he exhaled. His heartbeat stammered, and his eyes dilated fully. I hovered near his mouth, wanting with every particle to close that last two centimeters of distance, but I knew it would build the excitement if I waited. I licked my lips slowly. Kuta looked like he was in pain.

Good.

I tilted my head and moved in. This kiss was harder, more intense. If I'd thought the sensations before had lit my systems, this new onslaught ratcheted up the feedback to overload. I finally understood humans' desire for food. I hungered for Kuta's touch, for the movement of his lips, for when his tongue, at last, slid into my mouth.

I was immersed in Kuta and he in me. Minutes streamed by, and I gloried in his hands stroking my arms, his lips on mine, the warmth radiating from his body.

My damn internal alarm buzzed a warning. A definite life form moved toward us, low to the ground.

My sensors couldn't get any good feedback on what it was other than it seemed to be organic.

Whoever or whatever approached had best be prepared to face the wrath of Zee. I pulled back from Kuta, his eyes half-closed and his lips slightly swollen, lost in a daze. I hated ruining this moment, but I had to think of our safety first.

"Something's coming. I'm going to check it out." I stood and started into the brush.

"Wait for me. Remember we're a team." He scrambled up, looking less calm and together than usual. His body coursed with testosterone, and it was harder for him to suppress his biological responses than it was for me. I almost smiled. It felt good knowing I'd affected him as much as he was affecting me.

I didn't argue. If we were to be equals, I'd respect his wishes, and we would face whatever waited together. My internal systems hummed. With the walls between us crumbling, being on a team with Kuta, I felt filled up to the brim with positive ions. There were still things we needed to discuss, many, many things, but this was a nice beginning.

Following my sensor reads, I lead the way with Kuta at my heels. I turned up the insect repellant, which was a drain, but I wanted Kuta protected. The readings of life forms increased. I paused to examine our surroundings. Kuta squinted as if he could improve his average vision by doing so. Adorable.

"The signal came from here, but I can't pinpoint—" I heard the screeching a millisecond before Kuta. The foliage moved as if it had sentience. Visually, nothing was there. My still spotty scanners showed an unknown mass approaching.

"What the hell? It's rats! I've never seen that many," Kuta said.

I froze, stunned. Sifu feared rodents and had gifted me her exact brain pattern. I didn't know the precise reason why these tiny vermin were devils on four legs, but my body reacted by locking.

"Climb," Kuta yelled at me and shimmed up the nearest tree.

The rats had the ability to destroy my exterior, and if they gnawed deeply enough, damage my wiring and internal working. They were a true threat. Fear nailed me to the spot. A sea of rodents rushed me, so many I couldn't count, all with tiny, intense eyes and sharp teeth.

"Zee! Snap out of it and climb!"

Kuta's voice pulled me back from creating images of my body being consumed by rats, and I followed his instructions. The rats could ascend and attack, but they seemed focused on their exodus. A coconut palm leaned at a forty-five-degree angle to my right. I dug my fingers into the bark of the trunk and scurried up far enough to be clear of the vermin.

The rats continued to run as if they were being chased.

My breath came in pants again from my fear response. If it hadn't been for Kuta, I might have stayed frozen for too long. A dozen scenarios played in my brain in which I ended up on the jungle floor, dismantled.

Kuta settled comfortably in a crook of his tree, glancing between the rats and me.

After another twenty-two seconds, the flood of rodents subsided. Kuta made his way down the tree and walked over to mine. I had an intense desire to stay safe in the branches.

Damn human mind-mapping.

Kuta reached up and offered a hand to coax me down. I took it. Warm and supportive and strong. Just like him.

"Scared of rats?" he asked, not in a mocking tone, but a quiet, serious voice he reserved for quiet, serious discussions.

I could deny it. Retain my superhero status in his eyes. Blame a glitch. But I didn't want to. I'd always been honest with Kuta, and I wanted to keep it that way.

"Yes," I said.

"Me too."

I smiled, feeling better, but a few facts nagged my processor. "It's unusual for them to be out like that in the daylight. And they seemed to be running from something, but nothing was chasing them."

"I believe the shelter thing just got even more important. Let's find a good location away from the rat colony, and later we can explore. I'll need food soon."

Kuta would never in a trillion years admit it, but he had gotten a big dose of charisma and leader-ship genes from his mom. He took charge and made compelling arguments without being overbearing.

"You know, you could be a great politician some-day. Good ideas, great leadership."

He made an exaggerated gag face. Empirically, I knew it was true. But he had to realize it for himself. Or at least stop denying it.

"I need to thank you. That's twice you saved me," I said.

Kuta averted his gaze and ran a hand through his thick, black hair, shifting to the back of his neck, which he rubbed. "You rescued me from Facility F and battled a droid army to save me, so I owe you a bit more than that." He shook, and his face morphed from serious to happy.

"Come on, Zee," he said. "I know you can eat sun-shine, but I need more sustenance. We can scout for a good shelter location on the way back to camp."

Good plan. Part of me wanted to go back to our little lagoon and pick up where we'd left off. But there'd be other opportunities for that.

Unless.

A new thought process intruded. We may be discovered before that. A shot of fear and sadness threaded into my systems, slowing my movement, pulling my shoulders forward.

"Everything okay?"

I had to give him credit. He was acutely sensi-tive…for a human.

"Yes and no. I'm concerned about what will happen."

"We got the food, shelter, water—"

"No, not that. I mean… We have time to discuss this. Let's just make the most of it. We haven't got our primary needs covered yet, and I have a few wants I'd like to explore before we get to any more heavy talk," Kuta said.

I smiled a closed-lipped smile and nodded.

How many opportunities in my existence would I have Kuta to myself and be in a gorgeous secluded area? The odds were not in my favor. Being here with him was like hitting the droid lottery, and I wouldn't waste it.

I walked up closer to him, stepping over jutting, gnarly roots. We avoided the areas with the most vegetation and zig-zagged along the shaded path back to the beach.

We came to our camp and the area where Kuta had stacked fruit and coconuts.

I cracked the coconuts, and Kuta ate and drank. I knew he wasn't completely satisfied, but time slipped by quickly, and little in my DLed info told me about island living.

I shared it with Kuta as he bit into a purple mangosteen and spit out the seeds.

"So I have a list of things not to do. Don't build too close to our water source due to insects and away from the beach due to tides. Also, we need to consider if we want to be trying to signal passing ships. We could get lucky." Or unlucky.

Kuta spit another seed out and raised his eyebrows. "No talk of the outside world should also be on the survival list."

"Noted." I smiled and soaked in more power. I could ignore logic for a bit more.

We didn't talk. Together, as if we had some kind of internal coms, we walked up the beach and into the tree line. I led the way until I found the most logistically sound area. Shaded, free of evidence of vermin or predators, with materials to build, and a view of the beach. I motioned for Kuta to begin clearing the area, and I gathered fallen logs and sticks to use for walls.

It would be fine. I wasn't selfish for not insisting we look for a way off the island.

Kuta hummed and whistled while he worked. Even though he usually acted happy and positive, this version of Kuta had been harder and harder to find. He'd been unhappy with the constant moving and threats to his and his family's lives. Unhappy with his lack of freedom. Just unhappy. This break from reality had to be blissing him out.

I should mention how our energy would be better used gathering wood for a signal fire or searching for the rescue raft again. But I would let him have his moment. I would allow myself a moment, too.

We worked in sync. I gave minimal instructions. He intuitively knew what to do. I took on much of the heavy lifting, only pulling Kuta in when I needed help. I notched the small logs, so they fit together in a tent shape while Kuta used palm fronds to fill gaps and provide a makeshift floor. The structure was done in less than two hours. It would withstand rain and potentially a storm. There wasn't a door, but the breeze from the ocean was needed to help stabilize my cooling system. A positive emotion rolled over me. I may not be fully functional, but I maintained many skills.

The structure would last for as long as we needed, and I discovered templates for a more advanced shelter if we stayed longer. A positive feeling scurried through my system, and I attempted to categorize it. Not pride. More like hope.

Kuta fell back into the shelter. Lying on the stacked fronds like a bed, he put his hands behind his head and crossed his ankles.

"This is the life. Beach view and a beautiful girl." His eyes rested more on me than the beach.

I made a decision in an instant. The touch barrier had been breached, and our time was limited. We had accounted for all of his basic human needs. I joined him in the structure and turned on my companion protocols. I hadn't ever turned them on fully, and I really had no idea how they melded with my human-based processor, but as my Sifu always said—nothing ventured, nothing gained.

Crawling in what I hoped was a seductive manner, I snuggled up to his side, smiling, making eye contact, and increasing the pheromone levels in the air.

"I might be in trouble." Kuta laughed and scooted over to give me room but eyed me curiously.

I walked my fingers up his chest until I got to his face. His breathing grew shallow. I touched his chin and smoothed his face to tilt toward mine. His mouth was slightly open as if he couldn't believe my boldness.

He was in for more shocks. This was my chance. Perhaps my only chance to be with him. I took his mouth, kissing him hard and leaning against him. Full body contact. My sensors purred affirmative feedback through all my systems. I wanted more of this. More of Kuta.

His body warmed against mine. The places where bare skin touched felt electrified. In a good way. He kissed me, but not as fervently as he had at the lagoon.

His heart rate and heat level rose. His eyes dilated. He enjoyed my closeness, yet he pulled back.

"Why are we rushing? Let's relax." He pulled me to him, and I lay my head on his chest, listening to his erratic heartbeat.

Had I done something wrong? I quickly reviewed all of my DLed knowledge of intimate encounters. I had followed the correct protocols. He exhibited all the right signals.

All my human-minded worries spazzed out at once. Hard.

I was instantly positive I'd read the signals wrong, and I'd pushed too much, assumed too much, taken too much for granted. Maybe he wasn't attracted to me at all, and I'd foisted my affections on him. I wanted to roll into a ball and cry. My breathing became ragged, but I fought the urge to display these emotions. It would seem like emotional blackmail.

I was damaged. I was a droid. And I was a fool.

I pulled out of his grasp and exited the tent structure in a flash.

"Sorry," I said. "I didn't mean to presume."

"Wait! Zee! Wait. Let me explain!"

I didn't want to hear his reasoning. I'd DLed enough vidclips to know how the story went when one friend pushed another into a romantic relationship. Horrible and awkward and sad. I needed to gather my bearings and reexamine my situation.

My sensors caught Kuta following me.

"I detected something at the top of the ridge," I said. "I need to check it out. Alone."

"I just don't want to rush things. I really like you," Kuta said.

I didn't stop my forward path or look back. Kuta's vitals were still elevated but returning to normal. He stopped, returned to the structure, and dropped to the ground in front of it, cross-legged. If he said anything, I blocked it out.

I ran toward the cliffs and the highest point on the island. When I was back in the jungles of Thailand where I was activated, I always enjoyed spending time in nature in high places to soothe my cyber-soul. Back then, I hadn't understood my crazy fluctuations in emotions or strange clumsiness. I should've operated precisely. I'd thought I was defective.

Sifu eventually told me I wasn't just modeled on a human, like a normal military-spy droid. She'd broken every rule and patterned me on her own brain. Banned from having children, she'd longed to be a mother. So having an android with her exact brainwaves was the next best thing.

I wasn't her exactly. New experiences caused differences in personality and temperament, but I had her instinctual reactions. All the power of a droid with the awkwardness of a real teenager. Not the best combo. So even though I wasn't defective, I wasn't normal either.

I scrambled up the side of the jagged cliff. Even if Kuta tried to follow, he'd have to go around to the jungle near the waterfall to find a place where humans could climb.

But I wasn't limited to human methods. Even at fifty percent power, I leaped from handhold to handhold. I determined the density of the rock so I wouldn't choose a location that would crumble.

And even if I did, even if I fell, the thought of which sent a deep wave of bone-crackling fear under my skin, I would survive and, with self-repair, be fine. Humans only had limited self-repair.

Being a droid was wicked cool sometimes.

I thought of Kuta, and my momentary happiness plummeted. Why had I been so aggressive? All my DLs said he'd like my assertiveness. Now I was so embarrassed, I didn't know how I'd look him in the eye again.

My logic-based functions tried in vain to drag me from my assuming and conjecturing. Anything could be wrong. He might have just wanted to talk. He might be in mourning over Hassan. Even though Hassan was a royal jerk, he and Kuta had been friends for years. He'd need time to process those feelings.

But all these options paled in comparison to the fact that I'd been wrong again. Nothing my logic threw at me could steady my sinking emotions.

I was just a messed-up droid with human instincts. Sifu's brain mapping was too deeply ingrained for me to be logical. I'd have to let these emotions have their sway until they subsided on their own. I reached the top and surveyed the island. A cool wind brushed against my face. My joints loosened. Solitude was exactly what I needed to gather myself.

From my vantage point, much of the island was submerged. Since the mid 21st century, the sea level had increased exponentially due to a warming climate, or at least that's what my DLs said. Many landmasses had been totally consumed by the sea. Just fifty years ago, this island had almost been double its current size.

The sun shifted onto a lower longitude, and its rays reflected in prisms of light. I really shouldn't be away from Kuta for much longer. He had no protection from the bugs nor food for dinner. I really should be of some service.

And I should figure out what I'd done wrong instead of running away like an emotional child. My situation wasn't surprising. I'd only been reacting to real humans, other than Sifu, for six months. I had to give myself time to assimilate.

I found my first foothold and shimmied down to a small outcropping of stone. I noted a flash of movement at the far coastline and something bright orange.

Maybe it was the rescue boat that Kuta had used, or maybe it was some hint about Hassan.

With my damage, I could be wrong about what I'd glimpsed. I didn't want to get Kuta's hopes up if it would only lead to disappointment. First, I'd sweep the far coast. Then I'd square away Kuta's needs.

My trip down the side of the cliff went faster than the ascent. It was usually the case, but

excitement fueled some of my speed. I dropped two meters at a time catching onto the wall to slow my fall. The descent zapped some of my rebounded power, but I had something important to do—some concrete ways in which I could be useful.

And some girls just wanted a pretty dress.

I told my battling brain to shush and refocused on making it to the bottom in one piece. On my last leap, I landed with a jolt that sent vibrations through me and shook the ground. Small forest creatures scrambled for safety from the big, bad, android. I almost laughed, darted between the trees and leaped over roots, enjoying being able to let my power shine without having to pretend to be anything I wasn't.

On the island, I could be myself all the time, and no one would judge me. Kuta may not have felt about me the way I did him, but we always had a good rapport. Living here with him away from the Droids' Rights Riots springing up on every continent and the political squabbling between the Asian Republic and the rebels would be my idea of heaven.

The sun climbed high into the sky. I reexamined most of the coastline with still no sign of the boat. Perhaps my visuals had picked up something, but whatever it was had disappeared. Only a small, hard-to-reach outcropping on the north end of the island remained.

The good news was my self-repair had fixed most of my major systems, which infused me with renewed confidence in my abilities. Maybe Kuta was right, and we could live here away from the conflict and constant worry about assassins and kidnappers and war. For a while at least.

Here it was just me and him and a ton of potential for a real relationship between us. Out there, in the real world, it would be impossible. I was a droid. He was an important diplomat's son. We lived in two different universes.

A feeling like tiny anchors hooked onto me, but I brushed them away with the thought of Kuta's smile. I had him for now. And even in the real world, I'd be there to protect him. It wasn't a lot, but what did I expect? I was a droid and lucky to have any opportunities.

I reached the outcropping and realized the rocks shielded a small alcove. Kuta and I hadn't explored this area on our search. The alcove sheltered a narrow channel into the interior of the island. My scanners were good, but not good enough to penetrate 2.5 meters of solid rock. A strip of sand had grown on each side of the channel. The darkened cave waited.

I tried to turn on my hand illuminator and realized it had not been repaired yet. My night vision wasn't fully operational either. I still wanted to finish, so I could determine once and for all if the boat was still on the island.

My joints tightened, and my breath shallowed. Normally, I wouldn't be so leery of an unknown area, but a non-logical impulse surged danger warnings to my processor. Probably some silly non-reality based human fear, but I couldn't contain my response and moved forward with extreme caution. Limited feedback scrolled in. My scan reached a few meters in front of me, enough to keep me out of the water and give me enough warning to avoid rocky outcroppings.

I attempted to map my surroundings, like a bat using echolocation, I sent out waves of energy and received outlines of what lay ahead. Something strange reverbed off to my right. A blank area. Using the info that returned, I sensed a large mass.

What material would not scan, and worse, would absorb the energy, leaving me blind? I inched forward, reaching out with my hands until I connected with something soft, slick, and pliable.

Touch told me it was probably the boat, but how had it gotten here, pulled up onto land with some kind of shielding?

Maybe some internal system made it run aground, but I'd never DLed any info of a boat that advanced. And it shouldn't have reacted without a passenger. My unease returned, stronger and more persistent than before, almost like a hand touching my shoulder. The air moved like the breath of someone standing just behind me.

A scream broke the air, and I jumped. It wasn't coming from inside the cave but from down on the beach. I had reallocated much of my energy to pick up any distress sounds, and my caution paid off. The scream had to be Kuta. I bolted for the entrance.

There was no time to bring the boat. It was in a safe location. Kuta wasn't the panicking-screaming-overreacting sort of guy. If anything, he was the king of understatement. For him to scream for help meant something bad had happened.

I doubled my pace, leaping over obstacles, and using low-hanging branches to swing myself forward. I hit the watering hole first but detected no sign of Kuta. I veered my path and jetted for the beach.

A deserted campsite greeted me.

No more screams had sounded. Had my damaged systems engineered something? Maybe a replayed vidclip that I had mistaken for reality? I sighed. This must be what humans felt when they were going crazy.

Moaning tripped into my sound system. I followed the weak sound to the shallows where the vegetation grew almost all the way to the water's edge. Laying on his back in the shade was Kuta.

I knelt at his side, examining him for damage. I also sent a scan to the surrounding area. If we were under attack, I needed to be prepared, but the perimeter search returned negative.

Kuta groaned, and I gathered him up into my lap. All of my circuits pinged with tense, worrisome information.

Quashing my panic, I scanned him again, and this time I found the source of his ailment. A creature had stung his lower legs multiple times. I couldn't

determine what, but I'd conjecture it was poisonous. I couldn't figure out treatment until I was sure.

"Kuta!"

He moaned. I couldn't let him slip into some coma. I had to know what happened. I grabbed his shoulders and shook him. "Kuta Cheng! Tell me what stung you!"

Slitting one eye, he laughed weakly. "You're cute when you're angry." He writhed in pain, his eyelids fluttering.

The entirety of our time on the island skimmed through my processor. I'd been having fun. I'd <verb> what I'd always wanted, so I'd ignored every logical impulse to find a rescue ship. I'd foolishly been more worried about extending our time on the island than providing for Kuta's safety. Which put me in the position to get a delirious boy to tell me what stung him so I could apply some kind of first aid.

Sifu would have said, "*you dug your grave. Now lay in it.*" The thought wound my circuitry into a painful mass of fear, which morphed into anger.

No. Not today. There would be no graves. Not if I had a say.

"What the bloody hell stung you? You're going to die unless you tell me."

Kuta rolled his hands into fists and curled into a C position. I rummaged through every known dangerous land and sea creature. Many had horrible side effects, but not many of them were fatal.

I looked at his wound closer. The surrounding flesh blanched white as if the blood were retreating. A bad symptom.

As if there were any good symptoms.

I pulled Kuta up and into my arms again just in time for him to throw up the fruit he'd eaten into a fetid pile of goop on the beach. His eyes closed, and he shook, even though it was 31 degrees C.

I wanted to start shaking myself. I only had some minor DLs for human health. I was supposed to extinguish life or provide sensual pleasure as needed for my missions, not try to help someone of my own free will.

Damn the government for making me. And damn Sifu for making everything feel hard. I should just be wired to take directions, not to try to make decisions. This was too much to ask. Too much pressure.

But I had to do something. Kuta had no one else.

Whether I was wrong or not, I wanted to help Kuta. "Kuta. Hey, Kuta!" I shook him.

He opened his eyes again. "I'm so thirsty."

"I'll get you some water, but first, tell me what stung you."

He blinked and swallowed hard, coming back to reality a bit. His eyes focused on me.

"I don't know. I tried to fish so I could help, and I stepped on a rock then… it felt like a dagger jabbing into my foot. I didn't see anything. It was all I could do to get back to shore."

A venomous creature that looked like a rock and lived in the water. *No. No. No.* Of course, Kuta had to step on the *deadliest* fish in the ocean. A stonefish. I searched in all my DLs for treatments and prognosis. Every reference came back the same. Anti-venom was the only solution. Of which I had none.

Kuta's eyes slid closed, and his body jerked. I held his head to keep him from hurting himself while searching for treatment, natural antidotes, or other solutions. I found one reference to heated water, which slowed the poison and the deterioration of his flesh. Kuta's heart still felt strong, but if he was already convulsing, his time was limited.

First, heat water. I grabbed a medium-sized log and used the heat in my hand to hollow out an area big enough to put Kuta's foot in and filled it with water. Having droid strength was of definite benefit. The load was awkward but manageable. It took a few minutes to heat the water.

Kuta squirmed on the beach. He was about to hurt a lot more, but it would help to manage the poison while I deduced what to do next.

I lifted his foot and braced myself. I wanted to do literally anything more than I wanted to hurt Kuta. But if I wanted to extend his life long enough to save it, I had to try this treatment. I took his bare foot in my hand. Hesitating.

"Kuta, this will hurt. Brace yourself."

I submerged his foot. He stiffened at the heat and tried to pull it out, but I held it until he stopped struggling.

The foot swelled to twice its normal size, his toes like an overstuffed sausage. Dark red splashes tinted his skin. Two areas on the pad still looked white-gray. From my data, that meant the skin was deteriorating from the poison. The same poison coursed through Kuta's veins and compromised his organs.

Emotions tied my processes in knots. What would I do if I couldn't save him? What *could* I do to save him? The hot water helped, but he needed real treatment. And the only treatment resided in the raft on the far side of the island. I'd have to leave Kuta—who could have a heart attack or choke or anything.

My hands shook, and my breath grew ragged. I wasn't a med droid. I was a stupid companion droid tricked out to be a spy and twisted with all sorts of human hang-ups.

A human could allow herself to dissolve into panic. A real droid could just follow the logical path and not be constricted by complex fears of making things worse. But no, I was some weird mix of both, and my emotions and my programming slammed conflicting messages into my processor. I put my hands on my head as if that could keep out the repeating messages.

You could kill him. You have killed him. You're doing it wrong. You can't leave him.

Droid-logic kicked in. *Recon for the boat would give the subject seventy-seven percent survival chances. Proceed immediately, or chances of retaining extremities decrease exponentially.*

But leaving him here didn't feel right. I growled my frustration and pounded the sand. I had to stop fighting within myself. I had to act. My emotions and logic needed to work together.

"Kuta, I found the rescue boat. I'm going to bring it here. It has medicine and other supplies that might help you. Lie still. Keep your foot in the water."

He didn't respond but seemed to be in less pain than before.

I took off overland, trying not to look back and suppressing as much emotion as I could in order to function.

❖

Sifu would've been proud of me. I cut ten minutes off my time back to the cave. I didn't hesitate upon entering this time. My scan said nothing obstructed my path. I didn't have time to deal with a triggered human sixth-sense. I focused on avoiding the jagged walls and finding the rubber boat again.

The blankness appeared in front of me. My sensors still read nothing, but my audio picked up a low rasp like an inhale. A flash of repaired memory vidclip flared into my brain.

This had happened before.

I was suddenly back on the boat the night it sank. Wind battered me. I was on deck looking out at the water. I heard a scrape and an intake of breath. The blankness had been there. I lifted a hand and connected with a large object. The blow, blunted by my hand, struck my head. Instantly, I'd retaliated, swinging at the empty area. I struck something, and I saw him, pulling him with me as I tumbled off the boat.

"Hassan," I said.

My memory clip faded, and I was back in the cave. And it was too late.

An object struck the back of my head and sent a pulse of energy through me. Not a blunt object this time but some device. My joints stiffened. I tumbled forward into the water, my face, and upper body submerged.

My processes continued to function, but my body was useless.

I slipped forward into the water, and my panic rose. I didn't want to go out like this. Not when Kuta was injured.

And there was Hassan.

He'd damaged me. Probably so he could sabotage the boat. That part was still hazy in my recall, but it made sense. But all my revelations meant nothing with the cold water sucking me down.

How long would I last here until my battery finally gave up? Days, weeks, months? If I got even an inkling of light, I'd still be conscious, but unable to move. I had to get out. I had to save Kuta. I had to save myself.

"Malfunctioning, bitch-bot." Hassan stood directly above me.

My feet were still tenuously holding the muddy bank, and I sensed him move forward.

He'd shove me the rest of the way in, and I'd be lost. I told my hands to dig in and hold the edge, but it was like being in a shell. My emotions lurched between raw panic, fear, and anger. If I ever got my ability to move back, Hassan's days as a fully, functioning human were numbered.

He gripped my ankles, and I braced internally for the water's depths. But he didn't push me in. He dragged me back, grabbed my wrists, and clamped something on them. He repeated the action with my ankles.

My scanning didn't detect him, but I heard his movements. What was he going to do?

The object clamped to the back of my head released, and movement returned to my limbs. I jerked hard against my restraints. Fire licked through my wiring. He'd restrained me with some kind of electronic cuff.

"No use fighting," he said.

"What did you do? Why? Kuta is injured. We have to—"

"*We* don't have to do anything."

I couldn't see Hassan as he yanked me up and pushed me forward. I took a restraint-constricted step forward.

"Take me to him," he said.

I didn't know if it was a good idea. Kuta was vulnerable, and Hassan was violent. I had no idea of his intentions to Kuta. I stopped.

"Really, droid? You have destroyed my life, and you won't even let me go to see my best friend when he's injured? Not surprised."

My decision-making wavered between wanting to remove Hassan's head and wanting to help Kuta. Every tick of the clock sent the poison further into Kuta's system. I couldn't afford another internal argument. I'd do what I could to help save myself and Kuta.

Before I could say anything, Hassan shoved something with a rounded knob into my back again, touching my skin. "Maybe this will help motivate you." A jolt of electricity drove me to my knees and blanked out my processor. I almost screamed but could only manage a whimper.

Lucky me, I could experience a whole gamut of pain as well as pleasure. Good idea in theory. I could be motivated like a human. It worked just like human pain. It was supposed to warn me of potentially damaging situations and control me. But my programming took it up another notch because of my mind-mapping. Another gift from Mom. I tried to bring my thoughts back to Hassan. I had to do something before we went to Kuta. I had to make him listen.

"Meds." I bit the words out, trying to keep my vocalizations calm and even. I failed miserably. My voice shook with pain and uncertainty, and I hated myself again. Hated my weakness.

"What meds? Speak up, or I'll shock you again. I still haven't thanked you properly for the concussion you gave me back on the boat."

Good. I wished I'd let him drown in those massive waves, but I'd foolishly saved his sorry ass. "Kuta needs anti-venom. He was stung by a stonefish."

"He would. Not the smartest, that one. Fine, I'll make sure to bring the kit."

Relief flooded through me. At least Kuta would have a chance. Now I needed to figure a way to escape these bonds and get the jump on Hassan by the time we reached the beach.

I shifted to see what Hassan was doing, as he still registered as nothing on my scanner. I used my normal visual feedback to pick up an outline of him getting into the boat and yanking me after him.

The boat would be faster than shuffling along the jagged coastline.

He pulled out of the murky cove, and I got my first good look at him. A massive purple bruise swelled on his already large forehead. He wore a squint-eyed look of disgust, which wasn't unusual, especially when directed at me. He was just about Kuta's age of sixteen, but he looked older. They'd been friends for years. I had never really understood the allure. Hassan's surly attitude contrasted sharply with Kuta's lighthearted spirit.

I decided to try to get more information from him. "Why can't I scan you?" I asked.

He settled in the back of the inflatable boat, chuckled and sneered at me, an electric prod in one hand and the rudder in the other. "Wouldn't you like to know?"

Typical Hassan. Asshole as ever. He wore a long slick jacket that wasn't appropriate for a tropical island. I knew of prototype clothing that would provide scanning shields to protect privacy. It wasn't widely available and was expensive. How had Hassan, orphaned friend, sometimes bodyguard of Kuta Cheng, gotten enough credits for it?

It solidified my feeling about the shipwreck. He'd tried to hurt Kuta for some foreign power. I worked at my restraints, only to feel a sharp slap against my flesh.

Another laugh from Hassan. "You can't break them. No one ever has. The more pressure you exert, the more pain you will experience."

I checked my anger as much as I could without blowing a circuit. If I couldn't break them, I was at his mercy. And so was Kuta.

"What are you doing, anyway? Why did you blow up the boat? Why keep me functional at all? Who are you working for?" I shouldn't just fire questions at him. He would probably just smack me with the prod until I blacked out, and then I would really be in trouble.

He narrowed his eyes, from my questions or from the mist that spewed up from the boat's progress, I didn't know. He refocused on the horizon. The sun glinted against the water as if nothing bad could ever happen in this pristine, perfect place.

I begged to differ.

I cursed my lack of creative thought. I could throw together already known ideas, but any leaps required some kind of organic component I just didn't have. At least, the boat scuttled in the right direction with the medication.

The boat measured 2.48 meters by 2.48 meters. Not big, but I knew the design. Engineers jammed emergency boats full of survival gear, meds, sun shields, flares, and at least one super-charged transmitter for a distress signal. Kuta had said the radio was disabled, but it was our best chance of rescue.

If I could overpower Hassan, the chance for survival increased exponentially. But that was a big *if.*

Figuring out Hassan's motives consumed me. I conjectured that he had been hired by an outside force to end Kuta's life. But the fact he agreed to take medicine to Kuta belied that explanation. I reviewed my vidclip memory. Large sections remained blank from those last days and final moments on the boat. Hassan had appeared happier at the end, but I could be incorrect.

I wasn't great with deciphering human subtleties. Even with my companion protocols and human mind-mapping, it was more of an art than a science. And droids sucked at art.

The boat sped along the coastline at approximately twenty-five knots. We would be there in minutes, faster than I had run.

Even if I wasn't good at subtlety, I did have some pre-programmed negotiation skills. Perhaps I could talk Hassan out of his heinous plans.

"Why did you want to hurt Kuta? I thought you were friends. We can still work this out and escape the island," I said.

"I didn't try to hurt Kuta. Stupid bitch-bot. You don't understand anything. Now shut up before I prod you again. They would take you functional or non-functional, but I'll get more if you still work."

I tried to make sense of his words. If hurting Kuta hadn't been the plan, why set an explosion on the boat? And *who* would take me?

No one. No one would be taking me anywhere, and the only one non-functional would be Hassan.

We arrived at Kuta's location on the beach, and my nerves tightened my tendons.

I pointed to the tree line. "He's over there in the alcove under the shaded area."

Hassan grunted and aimed at the shore. Once we were close enough, he jumped out and dragged us up far enough to secure the boat. With the med kit under his arm, he approached the unmoving lump that was Kuta. I scanned him, my muscles winding tighter and tighter. I sent a prayer to Sifu's god that nothing had happened while I was gone.

I reached out. Sensors grasping for any indication of life. Of breath.

At last, I honed in on Kuta's vitals. His heartbeat. A wash of sparkling joy like a power bath rushed through me. He was alive. There was still a chance.

I struggled over the edge of the boat, tumbling onto the wet sand. Hassan leaned over Kuta, searching for the right treatment. I held back a scream that I had some medical training and for him to get his big, fat, buffoon hands off Kuta.

Logic quieted me. Hassan had the meds and intended to help Kuta. And this might be my only chance of escape.

I pulled at the wrist ties, testing their tensile strength. The electric force flared to life and snapped at me, searing my skin. My pain receptors throbbed.

Damn. Damn. Damn. If the feedback weren't so intense, I could probably break them, but my unique mix of human responses and droid programming conflicted. Again.

I couldn't just give up. I yanked, and it zapped me. A loud crack sounded as it rebounded against my metallic chassis. My body shook with the impact, vision darkening. I struggled to keep my processor functioning as my limbs convulsed.

Hassan hovered over Kuta, hypo in his bloated hand. The image rankled my nerves worse than the shock from my electronic cuffs. If I couldn't get out of the ecuffs, I'd have to escape with them still attached.

I crawled toward the forest. A rock or a tool could help with the bond if I could get there before Hassan noticed.

"Hey, hey now. None of that, Ms. Most-Wanted." Hassan grabbed one arm and dragged me up the beach to where Kuta lay. I quickly scanned his vitals.

Steady heartbeat, blood pressure still elevated but stable. It was hard to gauge his blood counts, but they too seemed improved. Yet he remained unconscious. Hassan had administered the medicine. But what did he have planned next?

Hassan removed the radio from the boat. His shielding jacket kept me from picking up what he was doing. I worked on my restraints. They seared deep ruts into my skin. I wanted to ignore the pain, but the feedback was too intense and fed by my stupid emotional chip. I laid my head against the ground.

What else could I do? The options scrolled out. None seemed plausible.

This was horrible. No way to escape. Just a hundred negative feedback loops of anger and blame and sadness. The main question circled again and again. What could I do?

No droid should ever have been given the burden of decision. I longed to be a normal droid with no conflicting emotions, no negative feedback, no decisions—just following my programming and shutting down at night.

Yet that wouldn't be satisfying either. Part of me liked the gooey emotions, the highs contrasting with the lows. The affection I felt for Kuta. I closed my eyes. Would I ever be some version of normal? Would I even have the chance to find out?

Two hours later, Kuta stirred. My wound-up emotions released marginally. Even though my scans had said he improved, I had still been waiting, watching for any sign of alertness. If the sun was my body's power source, Kuta was my emotional sun, feeding my need for joy on a daily basis.

My wrists throbbed with the aftermath of dozens of escape attempts. Yet the restraints held.

Hassan ignored me as if I were just some piece of equipment waiting for his use, an improvement on his normal behavior. Usually, he was openly hostile. My co-bodyguard, if I should even consider him that, kept his full attention on the damaged radio.

With his back turned, Hassan hadn't noted Kuta stirring, so maybe I'd have an opportunity to devise an escape plan or find a way to overpower Hassan.

I scooted closer to the fire and Kuta. Hassan had rekindled the flames with a kit from the boat. The island sweltered at the apex of the tropical afternoon. The fire couldn't have been for warmth. Perhaps for cooking or even some unknown sinister task.

My lack of creativity didn't stop my processor from dredging up images of various torture methods using fire.

"Kuta, hey, wake up," I whispered as loud as I dared, watching Hassan's back.

Laying face-up with fronds under his head, Kuta twitched slightly, his breathing became uneven.

"Kuta. Hey," I said. "We might be in trouble. Wake up." I didn't know quite what to say about Hassan. Kuta would be excited he lived. Possibly not give me time to explain that Hassan was the enemy.

"Hassan attacked me and tied me up. He destroyed the ship, too. I don't know what he has planned. We need to—"

Eyes still closed, he frowned—not a lot, but a defined furrow of his brows and a distinct downturn of the mouth.

"No," Kuta said, clear and slightly sad.

That took me off guard.

"He's dangerous. Listen to me, Kuta."

"I'm sorry, Zee. But you're wrong." Again, Kuta's voice was strong. Yet his eyes were still closed as if he couldn't bear to open them.

As much as I liked Kuta, this was not endearing him to me. Every military sense I had told me the longer this conversation continued without action, the higher the probability of Hassan realizing our plan and doing something to stop us.

"I know you're confused. But listen to me."

"Stop, Zee." Kuta opened his eyes and sat up with a low moan. "It wasn't Hassan who blew up the ship. It was me."

"What?" I reviewed what he'd said and replayed it. And replayed it again. Something must have damaged my audio inputs.

At that, Hassan turned and smiled at Kuta. No. No. No. This was wrong. Bad. And altogether not okay.

"Why?" I croaked out through a strangled voice box. My internal matrix had to be glitching. The blow to my head had shorted my visual and audio inputs, and I was watching a vidclip of someone else. Someone else in an upside down world where everything I knew was wrong.

"Freedom," Hassan said. "If NAR thinks Kuta's dead, there will be no more kidnapping attempts. No more risk. He'll be able to live a real life." Hassan's voice felt like a cheese grater against my emotional chip.

I hadn't looked over at Kuta. I hadn't dared. If I looked at him, and it was true, my opinion of him would be compromised. But I had to. I had to know.

I caught his beautiful face in my visual.

His head dropped; eyes averted. Shame.

A pain rebounded through my system so strong that it dwarfed the feedback from my arm and leg restraints. The place where my human heart would have been constricted until I wanted to scream. I wanted him to deny it. I wanted him to fight back. I wanted him to at least meet my eyes.

"You didn't tell me? Why? Because I'm a droid? Because I'm not good enough? I was sure good enough to kiss." I wanted to run away and slap him and hug him all in one strong wave. Damn, human emotions conflicted in some strong ways. I'd do none of it because the *chosen* one, the one who knew everything, Hassan the horrible, had bound me.

"Let her go, Hassan. Why is she tied up, anyway?" Kuta asked.

Hassan maintained his distance, his hands shoved deep into the pockets of his shield jacket.

"Zee," Kuta said. "Let me explain. I wanted to surprise you."

"You succeeded." I worked on my bonds again. I'd have given a body part to be far, far away from him, Hassan, and this wretched island.

"No. Really. I was scared you'd pick apart my plan, and I wanted to be free so bad. Then the blast went off too soon, and neither of you made it to the boat. It was my fault. And I couldn't tell you." He bit off the words as if getting emotional. His breathing hitched.

His meaning sank in and marinated in my brain. Hassan watched us.

"Hassan attacked me." I reshuffled the pieces of the mystery, and still, they didn't click together. That nagging feeling I'd experienced in the cave and in the forest picked at my processor. Danger. Danger. Danger.

"Who? Hassan? Why would he attack you?"

"Ask him! Ask him how he got that injury to his head. Ask him why I'm bound."

Kuta looked like a small child lost in a hurricane. "Hassan? Let her go, and we can contact my friends."

Hassan stood. The day had slid into twilight, and the sunset lit the sky a vivid purple behind him. With that backdrop and the fire before, he looked like the image of a demon I'd once DLed from the Renaissance. His dead eyes filled with the reflection of the fire.

"I'm just happy you're alive." Kuta stood up leaning heavily on his non-stung foot and made to move in for a hug.

Even with my limited knowledge of social interactions, I knew Hassan was not giving off hug-me vibes. He placed two hands on Kuta's chest and shoved. Kuta tumbled back and fell on his ass. I instantly bristled and struggled to stand. To fight back. To protect Kuta.

But I wasn't his bodyguard anymore. I wasn't even really his friend. He hadn't trusted me enough to tell me his plan. Or to tell me the truth afterward. I was just a droid.

I stilled and tried to tone down my emotions enough to function, maybe figure a way off the island. But the resounding pain of Kuta's lies still echoed through every thought, every impulse, every unnecessary breath.

Kuta sat up and narrowed his eyes at Hassan. His color still wasn't good. His tawny skin had paled, and sweat beaded his forehead, still fighting off the poison in his system. In a hand-to-hand fight, Hassan had the advantage.

"What's going on, Has? We wanted to be free. We're free. Now, all we have to do is use the coms to get a ride."

Hassan crossed his arms. "I'll never be free. Freedom is money, and that's what you don't understand because you've always had it."

The exchange enthralled me. This was riveting. I'd only seen their friendship. What Hassan hinted at was something else. Something darker.

"Hold on. Since we were boys, I've always shared everything with you—my room, my food, my resources. What have you lacked?"

"Lacked? Nothing. Until she came. I had to be the bodyguard. It was my job. It kept me from being a charity case. You took my job away and gave it to that thing. How soon until your mom kicked me out? I can hear it now. *Too much overhead.*" He paced, the hem of his long jacket flaring up.

I'd known Hassan hadn't liked me, but the emotion I read from him now was bordering on homicidal hatred.

"My mom thought of you as her child," Kuta said, sitting sprawled back in the same position that Hassan had left him, still too shocked to sit up. This wasn't good for him in his medical condition. He should be resting. He should be getting medical treatment.

Not that I cared.

"I was expendable," Hassan said. "You spent more and more time with the droid and forgot about me. I'd almost given up hope. Then you finally turned to me to help you get the explosives. You finally needed me. All I had to do was get rid of the droid, and everything would have been perfect."

"You were never expendable." Kuta's expression changed from shock to anger. "And what the hell did you do?"

"He attacked me," I repeated, my tone emotionless.

I sensed Kuta's vitals ramping up. His fingers dug into the sand, and his face twisted in a way I'd never seen. His expressions had ranged from happy to melancholy, but this was dark and angry and vicious.

"Then! Then!" Hassan was unleashed and didn't note Kuta's dark expression, or if he did, he didn't care. "I almost drowned, no thanks to you. When I came to tell you I was alive, I found you messing around with that thing." He threw his hand in the air, his eyes wide. "What the hell, Kuta? It's one thing to let it protect you but another to touch it. That's just sick. After I saw that, I knew you were beyond redemption. You'd never choose me over a sex-bot. I had to act. To save myself."

Kuta's jaw flexed. "What are you planning to do?" he growled.

Hassan smiled. There was no joy in it. "I have some acquaintances. And the droid has a large bounty on her. Enough for me to start over."

"Hassan! You can't! They'll kill her." Kuta scrambled to his feet.

I recoiled from the news as if I'd been pummeled in the gut. It couldn't be true. NAR government agents targeting me. The worst possible scenario for a runaway droid.

Cold chills ran over my skin, unease settled in me, and the deep desire to hide burrowed into my system. I didn't want to cease to exist. I searched for an escape, for any weakness in the bonds that I hadn't found the last 562 times. Still nothing.

"You can't kill what isn't alive." Hassan's nose wrinkled as if he'd smelled fetid fish. "And I'm sorry, but your attempt to fake your death is officially over. All I have to do is call in our exact location. You should feel lucky I'm not trying to collect the bounty on you, too. They'll take you back to your mama, droid lover, and everything will be like it was. And I'll finally be free."

Kuta fought to rise. "You don't know that. They could be assholes like you and try to cash in."

Hassan's lips pressed together. He took a breath and shook his head. "No, not going to fall for mind games. And stay down. You don't have a chance against me."

Truth infused Hassan's statement. Kuta realized it as well. He shook but settled down.

Only I could challenge Hassan, and my ecuff held tight. I wrestled until the pain nearly shut down my processor.

"I'm going to work on the radio," Hassan said. "Feel free to commiserate. It's the last time you'll be seeing each other." He laughed—a cold, hard, humorless thing.

Anger flared in me so hot that I nearly jumped him. Bonds or no. But my logic center pulled me back. If I waited for a better opportunity, waited until his guard was down, I might have a chance.

The radio diverted his attention again.

"Zee. I'm so, so sorry." If words could bleed, Kuta's would be dripping.

I didn't want to look at him. If I looked at him, I'd get caught in his gentle eyes. Not again. He was a liar.

"I never meant to hurt you. Zee? Zee, look at me." His voice wavered. I'd never heard him so despondent. So sad. "I honestly am sorry. I'll find a way to get you out of this."

The more he spoke, the angrier I got. He could do nothing. Just like me. "Shut up, Kuta. I'm just a machine. Can't be killed, so what does it matter what I think or feel?"

"That was Hassan," Kuta said. "I've never thought of you as less than me." He sighed heavily, and I sneaked a peek at him. Elbows resting on his knees, the setting sun lighting his coal black hair. He was a picture of abject shame.

"I just wanted to be free, and I knew you'd talk me out of it. I should have told you, and you would have talked me out of it. I almost lost you when the boat sank. I almost died when I tried to go fishing. I'm a complete failure at everything. But I'll make it right." He lifted his head and scanned the area, looking for something. What? I had no idea.

I couldn't help myself. I had to speak. "How will you make it right?"

"I'm going to stop Hassan." He whispered this, but I had a sick feeling Hassan was listening to every word.

Childish attitude. Nothing he did mattered. Nothing I did mattered. My inevitable destruction waited. No way out remained. I was a droid that was about to be scrapped, and that was my lot. I wasn't a real girl, no matter how much human brain mapping I'd been given.

If I had followed my droid protocols, I would have insisted on finding a way off the island. I would've searched harder for the boat. I wouldn't have been distracted.

If I'd followed my intuition and sensed that someone else was on the island sooner, I would've believed that tickle in the back of my brain telling me to beware, that someone was watching.

I was not a droid and not a human. I was something else. Something damaged.

"It's not going to work. Just let them take you back to your mother where you'll be safe after I'm gone," I said.

He cut me a look, and his head jerked. "That's not the Zee I know. The Zee I know never gives up. I watched you face a droid army to save me."

"But Kuta, I can't get out of these, and you aren't strong enough to confront Hassan. I gauge my odds of survival at less than twenty percent right now."

Kuta snorted. "There's a bit of my Zee. You're not going down like this. You're too special. Too important."

"Your Zee, huh?" I tried not to allow the words to stir my emotional chip, but that was about as effective as asking the sun not to rise. "Your Zee should have gotten you off the island like a good protection droid, but instead I got caught up. Because of my stupid feelings." The plus side was I wasn't going to have to bathe in recriminations much longer. The NAR military could just deactivate me or possibly blow me to bits. Or they could take me apart piece by piece while questioning me to find out why I was defective. That was an option too.

His face darkened and contracted, confused. "You really don't get it, do you?" He checked on Hassan, who was engrossed in setting up emergency lighting from the boats and scooted to me. He touched my wrist above the deep gashes. Pain jolted through my chassis, but I enjoyed the warmth of his hand on my flesh.

"You have the best of both worlds," he said in a low, harsh whisper. "The abilities of a droid and the soul of a human. A droid wouldn't have come back to Facility F to help me. It was completely illogical, but a human wouldn't have been able to combat the droid army. You're both. You just have to stop battling yourself and see what I see."

"And how do you see me?" I asked.

"Like a goddess."

"You don't mean that." How could he? I was lying on the ground, trapped.

"I do. The only thing you lack is confidence. You believe Hassan's crap. The reason he has a problem with you is jealousy. How could he ever compete with someone like you? You're basically superhuman. And that's why we have the droids' rights problems, too. Humans fear what's different. They fear being replaced by something better."

My processor stilled and tried to examine his logic, but my emotional chip buzzed with energy. The way he explained it, I did sound like a mythical creature with extraordinary abilities. Greek goddesses had a lot of power to help… and to hurt. I did too.

"But I've made so many mistakes."

"To err is human." He gave me a small conspiratorial smile. "My mom says it's okay to make mistakes, as long as you own them and try to fix them."

So, I could allow my faults to define me or find a solution.

All of his words were creating a swirl of contemplation, like a light switching on in the darkest part of me, reigniting my desires.

I wouldn't allow Hassan to win. I wasn't giving up.

"You're right. Giving up isn't in my programming."

He tilted his head, indicating a large fallen branch just behind me. "If I can take out Hassan, we can fix the radio and get help. He doesn't expect me to try anything."

"Kuta, you're too weak. He'll hurt you."

"Maybe. Maybe not." With a wicked smile, the old Kuta returned. Cocky. Brave. And stupid.

Kuta inched toward the branch, creeping, careful of Hassan's gaze.

I scanned his vitals. Better, but not near full strength. His blood pressure and his red blood count hung around the abysmal level. Surprise was his best weapon.

Hassan leaned over his work, concentrating while Kuta moved with a control and stealth that belied his injuries. He wrapped a hand around the branch, rose into a crouch, and took one step then another until he hovered just behind Hassan.

Kuta lifted his weapon.

Spinning, Hassan threw up a hand in some celebratory gesture, his thick, crude features pulled up in his idea of a happy expression. His face morphed into shock. Rage took over a millisecond later.

He launched himself at Kuta and knocked him backward. Hassan had no real training that I knew of, but he had his health, a dose of adrenaline, and plenty of pent-up anger.

"You were going to hit me? With this?" Hassan screeched. He snatched the club and swung it at Kuta. Kuta leaned back, barely keeping the blow from connecting with his face.

I crawled on my knees and elbows, still pulling at the ties as I moved toward the fight. Hassan raised the log again and fought to bring it down. Kuta's arm shook with the strain, his heart racing to dangerous levels. Hassan pushed down with his entire weight.

Kuta didn't stand a chance. If I could just throw myself at Hassan, maybe…

Awareness sizzled through me. The Cortex connection flooded my brain with information from weather to our exact longitude and latitude. My back straightened as my emotional chip doused me with a flood of useless panic.

The radio hummed to life and sent out a coms wave that I instantly translated.

As a military droid, I still knew all the basic code. *Droid Z12347, location 0.377170 longitude and 104.253547 latitude.* The message asked for the bounty for the fugitive and ended with Hassan's signature. All this had happened in .25 seconds. If NAR agents got that message, my fate was assured.

I could send a block if I reached the radio in time and clicked it off. Even if I had time to give it a solid kick.

But Hassan pressed the stick against Kuta's throat. Hassan's eyes bulged. He bared his teeth in some feral state.

Coughing, fighting for air, Kuta's face reddened. I remembered how the ocean had felt. Knowing I might not reach the surface.

Damn. Damn. Damn. If only I had twenty-eight more seconds. If only I weren't bound. If only I had a clone. But Kuta's throat would collapse in less than ten seconds. Hassan was putting his full weight and all his crazed energy into killing Kuta.

I'd worry about his revenge and the oncoming NAR forces after I saved Kuta.

Using all my strength, I leaped toward Hassan's back, shouldering him off Kuta, whose color had shifted from red to blue. My impact didn't have the complete desired effect. I'd displaced Hassan, but he remained basically uninjured.

He turned on me.

Me, who had no way to defend herself. Or to run. Kuta still lay gasping, clutching at his throat. He'd had some larynx damage, but I would say his chances of survival were good. If Hassan didn't have another chance to beat him.

Hassan snatched up the log. His hulking mass blocked out the fire and the sky and the world. I closed my eyes to stop my fear reaction from circumventing my logic.

I cursed my nature again. Fear didn't help. What Kuta had said replayed from my memory chip, *the abilities of a droid and the soul of a human.* Humans, in times of great stress, could call upon supernatural strength, mostly from the chemical adrenaline. I had the droid given strength to break my bonds and withstand the pain. It was my overloading emotional system that would cause shut down. What if I accessed the power of will to override my own system?

I was more than my system.

It might work.

My thoughts had taken a millisecond, but Hassan had already acted and brought the log down whistling at a speed of forty-seven km per hour. The blow would've damaged me potentially beyond repair. I rolled to the side and allowed him to bury the log in the sand two centimeters from my head. This impasse wouldn't last long.

I estimated the force it would take to break my bonds, dug deep into my desperation, and focused all my power into the area around my wrist. I wouldn't stop existing here. Not at Hassan's hand.

Crazier than ever, Hassan lifted the club and brought it down.

I yanked.

The force of the power feedback shook me. Every system redlined, telling me to stop, or I'd shut down. But I counted on my will, my desire to survive, to keep my higher processor working. My body convulsed, and I pulled again vision dimming. Red warning lights flashed in my brain.

Total failure imminent. Shut down systems.

I kept the force taut. With a lightning-bolt sizzle, the bonds on my wrist broke.

I lifted my hand to block Hassan and shoved him back with all the force in my chassis. He flew back and landed in the fire. I snapped the ties on my lower legs. This process took three seconds. And I was free and crawled toward the radio.

Kuta sat in shock, watching Hassan scream.

The coat Hassan wore may have shielded him from my scans, but it wasn't flameproof. The fire spread quickly, singeing Hassan's hands and upper back. He struggled to escape the flames.

All this occurred in 2.5 seconds. The radio was still a few meters away. There was a 1 in 1,000 chance I'd be able to connect and stop the signal. But damn it. Hassan might die. Could I exist knowing I'd caused another living organism to perish?

Leaping, I snatched him out of the flames and rolled him in the sand. He whimpered and cried, striking out at me as if I were the one causing his pain.

"Stop. Hassan. Stop!" I screamed.

He struggled out of my grip and raced away, flames still licking at him. I chased him and threw him into the water, holding him until the fire died. I dragged him out, much like he'd dragged me up the beach.

I wasn't gentle.

I ripped a piece of his clothing into strips big enough to bind his hands. I'd saved him, but that didn't mean I trusted him. Kuta stood again on unsteady legs and walked over to us on the beach outside of the circle of light the fire still provided.

"He sent a message to NAR, and I think they got it."

"You have to run. Hide. If they find you..." Kuta said, trailing off. "Zee, I can't tell you how sorry I am. Thank you for saving me. Again."

"We both had a hand in it. Equals, remember? You're right. I should go." But where? Not many places to hide on the tiny island. I still had a chance. It was time to say goodbye.

"Thank you, Kuta Cheng. You helped me more than you know. I hope we meet again."

I didn't wait for permission to grab him into a full body hug. It may be the last time I had to experience real human connection, so I wanted to go out on a high. He hugged me back, digging his fingers into me. "I don't want you to go. But go," he said, his voice shaky.

I turned, but he snatched my hand and pulled me back for another hug, giving me an eon to think about everything I was losing. My overworked emo-tional circuit blasted me again, and I forgot everything and just enjoyed the feel of his heart beating against my chassis.

"Go. Go," he said as he released me.

I ran into the forest, fighting the urge to look back, to get one more vidclip. If I did, I might not have the strength to run.

I pointed my processor to the task of creating a getaway plan and scrolled through the possible hiding spots on the island. Maybe the cave would give me enough cover to—my thoughts halted as my scanner reported really bad news.

A large force of humans and droids approached from the north. I backtracked, cutting through the trees that seemed to be closing in and reaching for me with long dark hands. The temperature on the island fell with the descending darkness, and I suppressed the urge to shiver, no energy to warm myself. I'd need it to save myself. If I could save myself.

For all Kuta's talk of superheroes and gods, I felt very small and had a strong desire to melt into the ground and hide.

Again, I turned my cyber brain to the problem at hand. The beach lay half a klick away. I could hide underwater in the shallows. My scanner jolted me, and I detected the presence of more individuals closing in.

Enemies surrounded me.

I sprinted toward the only spot my sensor evaluated free and climbed the waterfall Kuta, and I had visited.

Twenty-five soldiers—including military droids with armor, weapons attachments, and laser vision—swarmed. They locked on my location. My soft companion chassis didn't have a chance against those elite killing machines.

My military DL told me that escape was improbable. My human emotion agreed that I was the equivalent of burnt toast, but I kept moving. Something could happen to upset the situation. There could still be a way out.

I reached the top before the breeze from the helicopter became evident. It must've had a cloaking device and a sound muffler.

Two soldiers, laser blasters in hand, scrambled off the silenced aircraft and pointed them at me. Both clothed in head-to-toe jungle camo, face-shielding helmets, and black combat boots. They didn't appear human, not that it mattered. I raised my hands in surrender.

The smaller female wore the red bands of a troop leader on her arm. She turned on her com unit. "Subject acquired. Destroy or retain?"

A voice on the other end replied, but I couldn't decode the message. My hands shook as I considered snatching her weapon, but there was only so much one droid could do against a score of prepared adversaries. I forced my cyber brain to give me options. Jump? Run? Charge?

The leader fired before I could act. My body locked in place. She pointed a scanner at me, nodding. The other moved forward and sealed a circular band around my neck. It burned into my skin.

I knew what it was. I wanted to rip it off. But all my self-motivation had been removed. My weird mind allowed me the ability to think, but my body followed the command of whoever held the controller.

"Z12347, get onto the air transport," the female with the scanner ordered.

My body obeyed, zombie walked to the copter, and sat as obedient as a slave.

"The droid will be relocated to the front lines with proper restraints," the female said.

Frontline? Of the Droid Rights' War? On the wrong side. No. No. No. But as much as I hated the thought, I calmly sat in the helicopter as it took off and buzzed into the starless black night. I looked down to see a tiny, shrinking fire with two figures surrounded by soldiers. At least Kuta was alive and probably safe. No one would dare attack him with so many witnesses.

Calm descended on me. I still had a chance. I'd break their hold and gain my freedom. Maybe find Kuta again. Or just be free.

There was always hope.

I repeated the phrase as my new mantra as the helicopter headed toward the North Asian Republic and the front line of a war I didn't want to fight.

(Zee's journey will continue in Destroyed, *another installment in the Ionia Chronicles, available June 15, 2019)*

Our columnist, Julie Pitzel, has been a receptionist, radio DJ, bill collector, telemarketer, administrative assistant, community college instructor, and an expediter (a.k.a. professional nag). She's been involved in the Houston writing community for many years including two years as president of a local Romance Writers of America chapter. She writes paranormal fiction from a geodesic dome south of Houston, where she lives with her husband and a pair of cats. Most recently, her story "The Dance" was published in The Death of All Things *anthology.*

YOU READ *THAT?*: SHAME SHAME SHAME

by Julie Pitzel

A writer friend recently received a complaint from a reader because the heroine cursed. This book wasn't in a subgenre where only the bad guys use naughty words; it wasn't a sweet romance or inspirational fiction. It was romantic suspense written for an adult audience where the heroine is stalked and menaced and doing her best to stay alive. The reader didn't complain about sex between the hero and heroine. She didn't complain that the hero also used a few choice exclamations. But she was deeply offended that the heroine had a potty mouth while dealing with a violent stalker. She thought the character was a bad role model—seriously?

Reviewers have the right to their opinions. This woman didn't like female characters—especially school teachers—cussing. She's fortunate that the range of romance fiction is wide and there are plenty of authors and subgenres that can deliver fiction free of rough language. But, again, she didn't complain about the male character's language, so maybe it wasn't strictly the swearing that offended her.

It made me wonder if we expect better behavior from our heroines than we do from our heroes. How do you react to a romance heroine dropping the f-bomb? Is it okay for her to have on-screen/on-the-page sex with someone before she meets the hero? What about other damage? Can you accept a heroine who does drugs, drinks heavily, or gambles? What if she's deep into depression or PTSD and doesn't shower or change clothes for days?

Not very appealing, but I would wager we could find books published by major houses within the last few years that have heroes who display those traits. Other than the use of salty language, I doubt we'd find any heroines published by New York who engage in those behaviors—especially multiple sex partners. I can't think of an example of a romance heroine who has consensual relations with someone other than the hero in the pages of the book—excluding erotica.

Double standards are not new, especially in romance fiction. It hasn't been that long since heroines were expected to be virgins, unless they were widowed or (gasp!) divorced. If they were employed, it was in a traditional female role: secretary, waitress or teacher. And all too often the heroine would give up her job and home to follow the hero. None of those things are bad, but they were predictable and cliché, and part of the reason romance was looked on as anti-feminist.

The tortured recovering hero has been a standard romance trope since the days of the bodice rippers, but a tortured heroine is much less common. While the heroes grieved or felt guilt over things they did—think war hero—tortured heroines were more likely to suffer from survivor's guilt or things done to them, such as rape or abuse—aka victims. I'm not invalidating the fortitude and resilience it takes to recover from assault, only pointing out that women in fiction tend to be the victim more often than the transgressor.

In fiction, we expect to root for the protagonist. Most of the time, we want to like the main character and see that character eventually succeed. This is especially true with romance fiction where we want to fall in love with the characters, and we want the characters to fall in love with each other. If at the beginning of the story a character does something unheroic, it makes it difficult to root for them. It seems that male characters are given much more leeway for their bad behavior. An aggressive female character that we're supposed to like will usually do something early in the story to take away the sting of her take-no-prisoners attitude. She's supposed to be hard as nails, but the writer has to make her likable and that often means sacrificing some of her assertiveness.

Marvel's *Jessica Jones*, on Netflix, was a refreshing change for a tortured heroine. She's a broken, foul-mouthed drunk filled with guilt and pain because she killed an innocent person on purpose. Her remorse isn't because she was a victim, it's because she couldn't prevent what happened. But then *Jessica Jones* isn't romance. Most of the detractors of the show find her too intense, too off-putting, but there's a gritty realism to her actions and reactions that I enjoyed. And maybe that's what's missing from so many romance heroines—realism—characters acting like our friends and relatives and that woman staring at us from the mirror.

Romance is a bit of fantasy. We expect both heroes and heroines to be better, smarter, kinder, braver, and sexier than the people around us; but we also want to be able to connect with them. As much as we want to watch the fantasy, we also want the possibility of becoming part of that vision. We no longer see June Cleaver heroines doing housework in pearls and heels because nobody does housework in pearls and heels unless the cat barfed just before company shows up.

Our heroines have come a long way in the past couple of decades. They no longer sit back and wait to be saved. Often they're the ones saving the day. They can wield guns and welding torches. They're mechanics and pilots and semi-drivers. Isn't it time they're allowed to cuss as well?

Copyright © 2019 by Julie Pitzel.

C.S. DeAvilla writes award-winning science fiction, fantasy, and romance under another pen name. She has been a romance fan since she sneaked a peek at her mother's massive historical romance bookcase and fell in love with all the characters. She reads every romance genre—as long as two people are falling in love, she'll give it a read. Her favorite authors are Jennifer Crusie, J.R. Ward, Darynda Jones, Suzanne Brockmann, Sarah MacLean, and Christina Lauren. But she always has room for one more.

RECOMMENDED BOOKS

by C.S. DeAvilla

Title: *The Savior*
Author: J.R. Ward
Publisher: Gallery (Simon and Schuster)
ASIN: B07HWZKL94
Release Date: April 2nd, 2019

As a long-time Black Dagger Brotherhood fan, the character Murhder has fascinated me. It started when J.R. Ward mentioned the existence of another Brother who had gone insane and was still out there somewhere on the message board. His identity was well known and the other characters would mention him on the message boards, but the character didn't show in the books for several more installments and even then it was just a glimpse. So when it became apparent that he might resurface when hints were thrown in the last book, *The Theif*,

my inner fangirl went a little crazy. Ward builds mystic structures in her worlds that feel *real*. She teases out anticipation for years and delivers it in sips that feel like an oasis. *The Savior* stands up well considering it's a highly anticipated book of the series. Murhder returns to the brotherhood to sign papers for the property he's inherited, and it takes the Brotherhood out of a tight spot by keeping it out of the hands of an enemy. But Murhder has a favor to ask in return. He's been tracking down a woman from a research facility he attempted to save twenty years ago—an event that lead to his insanity as far as the members of the Brotherhood know. There's more to the story as there always is. Meanwhile Sarah is also working at a research facility and discovers that another lab is conducting unethical studies on a child and she breaks into the facility to save him. Murhder and Sarah cross paths and set in motion the events for the rest of the series. If there's one thing Ward does well, it's leaving readers wishing for the next book to hurry up and get on the shelves, even before they turn the last page of the latest installment.

Title: *The Bride Test*
Author: Helen Hoang
Publisher: Berkley (Penguin Group)
ASIN: B07CWDWZ1P
Release Date: May 7th, 2019

After the smashing success of *The Kiss Quotient* last year, I've been anticipating the next book by Helen Hoang. I had hoped for something that would return me to that same giddy feeling *The Kiss Quotient* gave me, but what I got instead was something even better. *The Bride Test* was a spectacular sophomore addition to Hoang's books. Funny enough, I'd downloaded the book while waiting for a tow truck after a flat tire. Most people would want that truck to hurry up, but I found myself—two hours later—still wishing that truck would be a little later so I wouldn't be interrupted. This book transported me easily from what should have been a crumby day to a fantastic love story that starts with an arranged marriage and a test our main character passes easily in the first chapter. Esme Tran (or My—the author switches from her Vietnamese name to her more Americanized name with ease) is the bathroom attendant at a hotel. Esme is comforting a crying woman when an older woman overhears and pulls her aside to ask her a few questions. See, this woman is looking for a wife for her son and she's decided her search is complete with Esme. And from the picture this woman shows, her son is supermodel levels of hotness. Esme is intrigued. The woman asks her to trick her son into marriage and Esme turns her down, but what Esme doesn't know is that she's passed the test. Soon she finds herself on a trip to America for the summer and a task—hopefully—to win over Khai Diep's heart. It proves to be difficult when Esme learns that Khai has sensory issues, can only be touched a certain way and likes his life exactly how it is. That sense of order keeps him calm. He's also convinced he is unable to love because of these neurological differences. Esme won't give up and not even Khai is immune to her compassion and adorable easiness with people. This was a heart-melting tale and unputdownable novel. Readers will fall easily for the characters and soon be pining for the next book from Hoang. A definite winner.

Title: *Autoboyography*
Author: Christina Lauren
Publisher: Simon and Schuster
ASIN: B06XR8Z9P9
Release Date: September 12th, 2017

There's a feeling only other book lovers will understand: when you finish a great book and crave that euphoria soon after. It sometimes seems like another good book may never exist, but you know that can't be true since you've had that feeling so many times before. And this is why readers become loyal to certain authors, we know they can deliver that emotion over and over again. Sometimes I'll save older books my favorite authors have written just for those times I'm desperate for a guaranteed excellent read. In this case it was a Christina Lauren book, *Autoboyography*. On a dare Tanner enrolls in a senior year seminar, where Provo High School students are assigned to write a novel in four months. No big deal he thinks, but he comes to find out it's so much more complicated than that. As is his life: complicated. He's a closeted bisexual in a very conservative Mormon town. So he's always hiding half of himself, and he decides to let that steam off in his novel project. He writes about an out-and-proud boy (with his family, at least) who ends up moving to a Mormon town and has to hide his sexuality at his parent's request until they can move back to a more liberal area. The story is a little too close to the truth and he needs a little help covering up the details so his teacher doesn't figure out his secret. This is where Sabastian comes in: super Mormon seminar TA who took the class the year before and sold his seminar project in a three-book deal to a major publisher. Tanner is instantly smitten and soon Sabastian is making a steamy appearance in his book and his life. It's clear Sabastian feels the same way and is only interested in guys, which puts a strain on his relationship with the church. And Tanner soon realizes if he turns in his project, he could out them both. But if he doesn't, he could get an F and ruin his chances at attending UCLA and getting the hell out of this unaccepting town. This book will take the reader places they don't expect. It doesn't shove the Mormon church in a terrible light completely, which makes it much more nuanced in how it handles a very serious subject. There isn't any ham-handed message, but it will challenge beliefs and family bonds and how important they are for young adults to thrive emotionally as well as spiritually.

If you're looking for something completely different in how a story is traditionally delivered, *Elements of Chemistry* is a good choice. Authors often experiment on how to best present a story and Penny Reid took liberal creativity in her *Hypothesis Series* with great results. *Elements of Chemistry* is actually three books. It's one couple's story, but broken into three arcs that each have a complete beginning middle and end. Each book is a full-length novel and the end makes it a romance as our characters have worked through the conflicts presented. For the purpose of this summary I'll only concentrate on the first book, *Attraction*, since going too far into each book would spoil it for readers—but just know that if long tales that give a story space to breathe and the characters to get to know each other in a more realistic timeline is your thing then this book exists and is waiting for your purchase. Kaitlyn Parker's life changes when she hides in her chemistry class's closet and overhears a plot against her chemistry partner Martin Sandeke. Seems like someone in his close circle of friends is attempting to drug him and sleep with him, hoping to then use it to blackmail him. Kaitlyn doesn't want to talk to her chemistry partner any more than needed to get an A in class, but her strong sense of right and wrong takes over and she tracks him down at the party where it's all supposed to go down and warns Martin. However, what she hadn't expected was that athletic, hunky, Martin has been looking for an excuse to get with Kaitlyn and now their relationship will never be able to go back to simple chemistry labs. I really enjoyed both characters and Kaitlyn's raw honesty to be true to herself and her standards every step of the story. It creates conflict for them throughout each arc, and it's totally worth it.

Title: ***Elements of Chemistry (Attraction, Heat, Capture)***
Author: Penny Reid
Publisher: Caped Publishing (Self-Published)
ASIN: B00UPU50EQ
Release Date: April 6th, 2015

Title: *Tyed*
Author: L. J. Shen
Publisher: Self Published
ASIN: B00YQDQ470
Release Date: July 1st, 2015

Blaire has the fortune of going through life as the less-successful twin. Her sister is a supermodel for a fancy clothing company and so she really needs for something to go right for once. Surviving and graduating college is her number one goal at the moment. So she has to ace her Journalism class. When she's assigned an article on MMA fighting—a sport she despises—she sucks it up and gets down to business. Mixed Martial Artist and soon-to-be Xtreme Warrior League champion, Tyler, takes an instant like to the sassy student journalist, but the feeling is far from mutual. He's got a big job ahead of him to convince her that not only is his sport worth the respect, but that he's worth taking a chance on romantically. This book is hot, hot, hot. The two main characters have some great chemistry and conflict, especially as Blaire learns more and more about Tyler and his past mistakes.

Andrea was drawn to Chicago to the famed Charlie Trotters Restaurant. There, Andrea was exposed to one-of-a-kind wine cellar in which she received one of the best wine educations in the world, tasting & serving some to the most rare and most special wines ever produced. She worked with some of the world's top ingredients, Chef's, Farmers, food lover's and wine aficionados, but homesick, Andrea returned to Santa Fe, NM, where she was Partner & Head Chef at Rasa Juice Bar & Ayurveda. Andrea received many rave reviews and won the Local Hero Award two years in a row for her organic, plant-based café. Her attention to detail to her beautifully plated and delicious food is enhanced with the love and care she infuses into every bite! She is currently the Owner and Chef of The Temptress Private Chef & Catering operated out of her home town of Santa Fe, NM.

THE TEMPTRESS PRESENTS: FLUFFY GLUTEN FREE WAFFLES

by Andrea Abedi

Breakfast is one of the most important meals of the day. It is highly important for many reasons. It not only replenishes the body's glucose levels, it also provides essential nutrients to keep energy levels up during the day. Gluten free Waffles are the perfect way to show your love how much you care. This extra fluffy recipe will start your day off right with your partner—who doesn't want to be surprised with breakfast in bed?—and nourish you at the same time!

INGREDIENTS

2 cups gluten free flour blend

¼ teaspoon xanthan gum

2 tablespoons sugar

1 ½ teaspoons baking powder

½ teaspoon baking soda

½ teaspoon kosher salt

2 eggs at room temperature, yolks and whites separated

3 tablespoons virgin coconut oil, melted and cooled (or a neutral liquid oil, like vegetable or canola)

1 cup plain whole milk yogurt

6 fluid ounces milk, at room temperature

1 cup whipped cream

fresh fruit

DIRECTIONS

1. Preheat waffle maker

2. Get all ingredients out. This is called *mise en place* (to put in place)

3. Measure them all out.

4. In a large bowl, place the flour blend, xanthan gum, sugar, baking powder, baking soda and salt, and whisk to combine well.

5. In a separate bowl, whip the egg whites with a hand mixer (or in a stand mixer fitted with the whisk attachment) until stiff (but not dry) peaks form.

6. Place the egg yolks and oil in a separate large bowl and blend with a hand mixer (or in a stand mixer fitted with the paddle attachment) until creamy. Add the yogurt and milk, and blend until well combined. Add the dry ingredients from step 4 and blend again. The mixture will be smooth and thickly pourable.

7. Fold the beaten egg whites gently into the large bowl of batter until only a few white streaks remain.

8. Pour or scoop about ¾ to 1 cup of batter into your prepared waffle iron (more or less depending upon the size and shape of your iron) and spread the batter into an even layer. Close the lid and cook until steam stops escaping from the waffle iron—between 4 and 5 minutes, depending again upon the capacity of your waffle iron.

9. Remove the waffle from the iron and serve immediately. Repeat with the remaining batter.

10. Top with whipped cream, maple syrup and any fresh fruit to you desire.

11. If you do not serve each waffle as soon as it is made, refresh the waffles by placing them in a toaster oven at 400°F for about 3 minutes. Waffles can also be cooled completely, wrapped tightly and frozen, then defrosted and refreshed in a similar manner before serving

Enjoy!

xo

CLOSING EDITORIAL

by Tina Smith

It's summertime and, man, can I feel it here in California. It's hard to believe, for the first time when putting together an issue, the weather reflects what it will be when the next issue publishes. August promises to be a hot one (as is May, when Lezli and I started selecting what stories would appear on these pages—and many stories were read even before that!). It takes a lot of time and careful consideration, but we're sure we know what *Heart's Kiss* readers want: more romance, for one. And we've got that coming your way in the October issue, too.

Kathryn Nolan will be appearing with an exclusive novella just for our readers—she's a hot new writer and if you've not read her other works, I think *Queen Cleopatra and the Baseball God* will be just enough to get you hooked. (Warning, you could go broke buying out all her other novels for your hungry e-reader.) We'll also have more stories by authors you love who frequent our magazine and Lezli interviews Darynda Jones. Thank you for your support and readership—we love fans of romance, and *Heart's Kiss* readers especially. Have a great summer and we'll see you in October.

www.ingramcontent.com/pod-product-compliance
Lightning Source LLC
Chambersburg PA
CBHW080904120626
46555CB00008B/2943